Collectables	5
The Web	23
Hole 13	33
Well-Seasoned	47
The Drone Rift	61
Dark Images	77
Cyber Human	97
Side Effect	109
Them	139
Enhanced Feelings	151
I'd Give Anything If	169
What's For Dinner	195
The Fountain	201

Ever since I watched an episode of "Nightmare" on television when I was a child, about 6 or 7 years old. The scene that stuck with me was about a frightened man that had crawled into his bed and covered his head to escape a ghost that was chasing him. The ghost that was after him still came through the covers.

I have been enthralled with the macabre. I like writing those stories that may end or may not. Stories that also make one's imagination follow into my macabre imagination. Looking at certain items or sometimes a person or even a conversation creates a story in my mind.

Enjoy these stories-let them tickle your imagination. Maybe they will be an encouragement to write your own; but be careful of what pen you pick up to write with, you never know. Maybe they will invade your sleep......

Collectables

The late afternoon temperature in Rossville was about 80 degrees. A breeze was blowing from the southwest about 10 to 15 miles per hour. The sky was a bright blue with a few floating white fluffy clouds. The people in the small town, were ready to end another day of daily activities. Although it was an older town, several of the buildings had been renovated with newer and more modern designs. Sidewalks were patched where needed but very few were replaced with new. It was a slow-paced town as some called it, where no particular person seemed to have a sense of urgency.

A young man, tall and lanky. Looking like he had missed a few meals when he was a young boy was sitting on a well-worn wooden bench. Worn blue jeans, an older stretched out V-neck t-shirt and well-worn in shoes, the man was visibly staring down the street at an old store that he liked to visit. The store was in an older building that sold antiques, some used items and an odd assortment of old second-hand items and things the owner called in his gravelly old voice "mics stuff". The building was located at the corner of the next street where the young man was currently sitting. The owner of the store had told him once that "someday" he might have it painted but he really liked the rustic look.

Mark Richards got off work from the grocery store at 4:00 where he currently worked in the meat department. Looking at his watch, and noticing that it was almost half past 4. Surprised that he had been sitting on the bench outside the grocery store for almost a half an hour where he had just been looking around and enjoying his surroundings and the wonderful weather, not to mention the few minutes rest from being on his feet for 8 hours straight. He Stood up and quickly readied his gear to start walking across the street toward the park.

    His favorite bench was in the town park next to the "main street" of town. Even though the name of the street wasn't "Main", it was what everyone called it due to all the main stores that resided on it. This bench was his particular favorite because it let him see many different items to capture like the many types of different people, numerous mode of transportation and lastly by no means the least, the beautiful scenery.

    Closing his bag, he reached down and swung his backpack, which was filled with all his drawing gear over one shoulder. His drawing paper which was often scraps leftover from the store where he worked; often because his pay was just above minimum wage, and he used whatever he could find. Inside his bag he also carried a small black plastic footstool that folded up small enough to fit in the backpack.

    When he got to the park bench, he pulled out his stool. Putting his feet on the stool he formed a slanted desk with his legs and grabbed his pencils and charcoal. Where he placed them on his homemade desk. Some of the pencils were of different colors. He had some gray plain pencils of course, but he also had found some natural earth tones, some reds that matched the surrounding building and some greens that almost exactly matched the color of the park grass. A few had been sharpened to a broad point with a pocket knife that he carried mostly just for that purpose.

    Before he began drawing, Mark would observe his surroundings until he found something that really piqued his interest. Today he decided to draw the park from this particular bench. First thing though, he had to turn the bench around, facing inward toward the center of the park, fortunately for him the benches were not bolted down. Not so fortunately for the park department as a few of the benches would go missing or end up in odd places like the roof top of a near-by store when some kids had got bored last year. When he was done, he would always turn it back to where it was supposed to be. His particular favorite bench sat on a small cement slab about ten feet in from the curb. Observing the park, he looked down the street to both his left and to the right. He noticed a row of Redbud trees, in line with the bench that he was on. All four edges of the park were built the same way.

    From each corner was a sidewalk leading to a large fountain in the middle. On the side opposite the fountain from where he was sitting were some swing sets for the children, a slide, and a merry-go-round. As he watched a few young children playing, he observed that the houses lining the opposite side of the park where he was sitting were old. Not just one, but all of them. They had been well kept, like they were there for show. This was one of the reasons he liked to draw them. The main reason though was the architecture.

The gables and the fancy windows. There were so many things he could draw from this advantage.

Behind the bench where he was now sitting, was the main street. Beyond main street was the parking lot for the grocery store. To the right was the small-town lumber yard with the large open stalls in the back. Further down the street beyond the lumberyard, there was a small dry lot that was fenced in with a few cattle in it.

The two-story farmhouse on the far side of the pasture that had been there almost as long as the town itself, which explains why it was now within the city limits. The siding was very weathered and in desperate need of paint. There were two old buildings behind the house. One was what looked like the tool shed and the other was a small chicken coop. Their structure was in the same weathered condition as the farmhouse.

Mark lived in an apartment above the grocery store. He had never been married. Being 22, he figured there was plenty of time for that. He did date once in a while. He was in good shape, kind of athletic and some of his dates considered him to be rather handsome. Mark was six foot and weighed around one ninety. He had two passions that kept him from doing a lot of dating. One was drawing and the other was the antique shop down the street, where he spent an abnormal amount of time. Most guys his age would be fishing, hunting, or just going to the bigger city. He was more into the antique shop than he wanted to admit. It seemed as more time passed, the less he drew and the more he spent his spare time at the shop.

Every once in a while, he would reach inside his shirt and hold a miniaturized dreamcatcher made ito a necklace in his hand as he was thinking about what to draw. He remembered back when his dad gave him the necklace, which came from one of his dad's old friends. His dad also told him the man owned an antique shop in a small town, a couple hours away. He had repeatedly asked his dad where the town with the shop was located. His dad always replied with, "Someday I will take you there." His dad had given the necklace to him for his twenty-first birthday and he thought Mark would really like it. The only time he would remove it was when he was going to take a shower.

As he sat there, he stared at the scene far beyond the parking lot. First, the creek, then the forest, and finally, many miles away, was a large mountain range. The peak in the middle had a small snowcap on one side. He thought about drawing it, but on the other hand he really wanted to go to the antique store and see if Charlie, the antique store owner, had received any new items for him to look at.

One time he had asked Charlie where he had found all his stuff, but Charlie would just cock his head, stare at him and not say a word. He would hold up his index finger to his lips, smile, and walk away. Charlie was an elderly man and except for his customers, usually kept to himself. His hair was already white and he knew he couldn't keep the shop going to many more years. His joints would ache and his back would hurt most of the time. But he just kept going. Besides, he enjoyed the visits from Mark.

Putting everything back in his backpack Mark stood up and put his arms through the straps. Maybe he would draw another day. After turning the bench back in its original position, he briskly walked across the street in front of the grocery store as to not get run over. He noticed the time on the bank clock. It was almost 5 o'clock and he knew he better hurry down to the antique store. Charlie would close his store at six and that would only give him an hour to look around.

Walking down the street towards the antique shop, Mark was weaving back and forth to avoid running into people. He could hear music coming from the local pub. As he walked by, he could hear someone getting pretty loud; either trying to get his point across or just having one to many. Next to the pub was a hardware store where Mark shopped sometimes to get items to fix something in his apartment. Mostly screws, nails, light bulbs, etc.

Across the street from the hardware store was a lonely little flower shop. He overheard a conversation, that they may close soon due to the lack of business support if it didn't change. He had always thought the town was too small to support a flower shop, but people do have dreams. Down the street next to the hardware store, was a home town style restaurant. He had eaten there several times. Mark thought the food was pretty good, especially their breakfast menu.

Across the street, was the gas station or convenience store, as some called it. It was more than a place to fill your tank; it had a little bit of everything- cold drinks, bags of chips, lottery tickets and shelves stocked with high priced essentials for people that forget to grab at the grocery store. The neon sign above the door flickered occasionally, buzzing softly, casting a dull red glow onto the pavement below. Past the gas station, was a small parking lot, and lastly a side street. Beyond that was a hill. At the bottom of the incline, was the creek that wound around the back of the town. There was a bridge at the end of the main street, the street that he was currently on. This crossed over the winding creek. Main street then turned into highway 22 which disappeared into the forest.

    Mark could smell the aroma of some bacon and pancakes coming from the restaurant. Thinking that someone ordered some of his favorite breakfast food made him think he might grab something on his way home. He absolutely loved their biscuits and gravy. Marks mouth was watering as he continued past.

    Next up was Charlie Harris's antique shop. He had painted on the right side of the front store window, "This and That". Charlie had told Mark he didn't know if he was going to keep that or put up some different words. Finally making his way to the front doors, Mark took hold of the door handle and heard the bell ring as he opened the door, alerting Charlie someone had come in.

    "Ah, Mark, just the person I wanted to see!" said Charlie as he limped up to the front of the store as he tried dodging items on the overflowing shelves.

    "Oh, really?" replied Mark.

"I'm going to close up shop early, say an hour early. However, I have something to tell you and also some items to show you." said Charlie as he turned the OPEN sign to CLOSED and locking the front door.

"Come with me young man," added Charlie, grabbing the strap on his bib overalls and tightening it up on his shoulder as he limped along. Mark knew he had a limp, but never inquired why. Charlie most likely would not tell him anyway. He was pretty private about a lot of his life. He thought it might have been from his time in the military. He figured that Charlie had served in some form of armed forces by the air of patriotism he had towards some of the military items he had in the store. Heading towards the back of the store, Charlie began to tell Mark what he had on his mind.

"I have known you for a quite some time now. I have no family left, I'm 68 years old and I would like to retire, I'm old enough. There is no one else that I would trust my things with, so I'm asking you if you would like to take over the shop when I retire? My health hasn't been the greatest lately and I want to get this settled so I can have peace of mind. I have known you for what seems like a lifetime with your dad telling me about you. I thought about it carefully and decided. That is, if you want it?" said Charlie in a questioning voice. "I talked with your dad several years ago. He said when the time is right, you will know, you ask him. I will leave it up to him."

At first Mark was awestruck, looking like a little kid, his first time in a candy store. He didn't know what to say, not believing what he had just heard.

"You can take some time to think it over if you like." added Charlie.

"I don't need any time. Absolutely, I mean, yes, a thousand times, yes! I'd love to take it over for you," said Mark with a huge smile.

Charlie extended his hand and said, "I'll see about making it legal. Tomorrow I will call my lawyer and make an appointment. Then we will go together to sign the papers, ok?"

"Really? Sure", was all Mark could say. He was kind of in shock, but his insides were jumping with joy.

"Ok, now that that is settled, I want to show you some items that I call 'Very special'."

They headed back through the store where the shelves were as high as Mark's head. There were items covering the shelves and also dust, a lot of dust. Mark had offered to dust for him but Charlie refused. He said the dust makes the newer items look older.

Charlie didn't move too fast anymore. He zig-zagged through shelves of toys, tops, buckets, lanterns, and mirrors. They ended the trail at the back of the store where he reached up and grasped his old hand around a coat hook on the back wall between two of the shelves. Looking over the should as best as he could, Charlie gave a mischievous smile and said "watch this!" Giving the coat hanger a twist, they heard a soft click. The stack of shelves next to the one with the hanger popped open on one side, like it was on a set of giant well-oiled hinges.

Charlie then pushed on one side and the whole shelf spun open revealing a spiral staircase going down into the darkness. Reaching along the interior side wall, feeling around the wall he found the light switch. He made the switch snap to life and an ominous glow came from below them. This in turn caused the stairway to become dimly lit. An odd thought came to Mark's mind as he thought to himself, 'maybe a higher watt bulb would help.'

    Stepping onto the stairwell, the pair of them headed down the stairs. Mark taking in the situation like a little kid going to his first amusement park. Slowly making his way down behind Charlie, Mark couldn't help but notice the walls were very smooth. There were no cracks or crevices that he could notice from the dim light. Three steps from the bottom, Mark slowed his steps. He was in awe at the sight. There were several antiques that he had never seen. It was like a whole new world. There were cardboard boxes, wooden boxes and even some old metal barrels with snap lock rings sealing the contents. Most of the items were coated in an old age dust blanket; appearing that they haven't been touched in years.

    Charlie broke Mark's trance by starting to explain about the items in this room. "I haven't gone through even half of these items, Mark. But for example, take a look at this case." Charlie started explaining as he reached for a metal case about five inches long and three inches wide, and black with a hint of rust. The bottom had part of a label left which was unreadable. The case Mark thought he recognized the shape was a glass case, and it could possibly contain a pair of glasses. Charlie resumed his talk, opening up the case and lifting a pair glasses up towards his face, "When you put these glasses on, it makes things appear that were not there, but were there."

After Mark's puzzled look, Charlie explained. "Ok, for example, go back upstairs and get one of your drawings. It not only works on paper, but also on pictures taken with a camera."

Quickly running up the stairs, dodging all the overflowing shelves, Mark retrieved one of his drawings of the store front and made his way back down to the basement. "How's this?" he asked as he handed it to Charlie.

"OK, this is perfect, now put the picture on the table," said Charlie as he brushed the dust off a crooked little card table. Making the table wobble with the slightest touch of his hand, cleaning off the top.
"Ok, now, put the glasses on and look at the drawing."

"Why?" said Mark curiously.

"Trust me, you are in for a treat." Charlies' face was lit up with a giant toothy grin, eyes sparkling with excitement, bouncing slightly on his toes, caught between joy, anticipation, and the anxious hope that it would be received with the same enthusiasm.

Mark put the glasses on and looked at the drawing. Quickly pulling them off his face. "What was that?" he said to Charlie, rubbing the side of his head from the slight tingle he felt when the glasses were on.

"Calm down Mark. Most of these items in this room are "special". Take those glasses for instance. I read the paper that was tucked inside the case. It said when one puts the glasses on, they somehow sense or read the mind of what the wearer was truly seeing. They seem to focus on that item. I don't know how it works but it does. I've tried them several times".

"Where did they come from?" asked Mark.

"It's like most of the items down here in this room. They have been here since I inherited the store from my dad, who got it from his dad, who got it from his dad, and so on down the line."

Mark looked at him with a questionable frown.

"How did they get here?"

"That is a good question. I asked my dad the same thing and he told me they were brought here. Now, I am going to tell you a secret. Have you noticed that some of these items have very little to no dust on them? Well, it seems that when I come down here to sell something, sometimes something else will have appeared that was never here before. Oh, before I forget. There is one item that my dad told me that his grandpa received by hand. Seems that some figure came into the shop and placed it down and just left. I've caught glimpses of that figure down here. Dressed in a large robe with the hood down over, well what I guess was the face. I watched as he put his, I also guess was his arm, out in front of him and an item would just appear. In fact, I think some of the items that left from down here he, or it, has returned them. No words were spoken or money exchanged. He just turned and vanished. dad said they couldn't see his face either. He left that projector over in the corner, too. Been there ever since. But, now, back to these glasses. I have little to no information about these items, or what strange power they may have or where they come from.

Mark's face had a cross between questionable and excited look.

"Ok, back to the glasses" Charlie continued. "What do you see?"

"Well, I saw people in my picture that I didn't draw, but I remember them being there. I don't draw people because no matter how hard I try; I just can't get the facial features right."

"Right, you have to be careful, I don't know about the power of these items in this room. Some may be very dangerous, some who knows," added Charlie changing the subject once again.

Mark was in awe. There was just so much to take in, right now.

"There is one item in here I'm sure you will enjoy. There is a quill and a leather pouch that contains ink. I don't know the details on them but I figured since you like to draw, you could find out more about them on your own, just be careful," added Charlie. "This place has a lot of secrets" ...

"I'm getting kind of tired now and it's closing time. We'll discuss more when you come back tomorrow" Charlie sighed.

Was I Dreaming?

"Mark, Mark, Mark, wake up!! We have to get going. It's a two-to-three-hour trip to Rossville Arkansas. You and your dad have something you have to do. We will explain on the way there.

Mark had come over to his parents at their request the night before to help them with something and ended up sleeping on the couch in the living room. It wasn't too bad of a sleeping arrangement, and breakfast was always included.

"Charlie is one of your dad's oldest and dearest friends. He has been talking to him regularly, once a month, if he remembers to," added Mark's mom.

"Did you say Charlie?" asked Mark.

"I had a dream last night and an old man named Charlie was in it," he said with a grin, as he pulled the dreamcatcher necklace around in front of his chest.

George reached up and took the keys down from the hook and placed them in his pocket. His mother was filling some containers with tea to take with them.

"Come on Mark," said Susan, as she grabbed the three containers that housed snacks for the trip.

Mark slowly pulled himself out of the house and all three headed for the vehicle. They backed out onto the street and his dad turned the car towards Rossville, Arkansas. Mark started telling his mom and dad more about his dream on the trip. He started by describing the main street and the park.

Mark's dad, George, looked up in the mirror and with a confused face, stared at his son for a few seconds before looking back at the road. He glanced over at his wife with a questionable look. She just shrugged her shoulders.

"Son, I don't know how, but you just described the town we are going to. "The only thing is, we have never taken you there. I don't know how you described it so well. You said that was in your dream?" asked George.

"Go on son, anything else you remember about the dream?" he added.

Mark described the creek that circled around in back of the town. The cattle lot, old farmhouse, forest, parking lot, even the snowcapped mountains. After he was done, there was a silence in the car for several miles.

Susan, Mark's mom, started to say something. She had seen the town about twenty-five years ago. From what she remembered, every detail Mark had said, brought back the memory of the town.

However, George put his finger next to his lips and told her to wait. He pointed ahead. There was the sign, Rossville city limits.

As they drove down the main street, Mark was in a trance. "I may have to move here," he thought. "It would really be a dream come true," he continued to think to himself. At the same time, he was confused about the dream and reality seeming to be one in the same.

They stopped in front of the antique shop. There it was, Charlie's, "This and That." A few minutes later Charlie stood in the doorway.

"Mom, that's exactly the old man that was in my dream", said Mark getting out of the car. Now he was really curious to see what was in the shop.
"Watch what you say son, Charlie and I are close to the same age," said George with a grin.

Mark walked up to the store doorway with his dad. "Charlie, I would like to introduce you to my son, Mark. Mark, this is Charlie Harris." Each extended their hands to shake but when Charlie's hand touched Mark's, both were jolted with a mild shock.

"George, did you give it to him? Does he have it on now?" asked Charlie as he rubbed his hands together.

"Sorry, must have been some static electricity." said Mark as he was trying to peer in the doorway.

"Are you sure that thing is safe enough for him to wear?" asked George.

Charlie didn't say anything, he just shrugged his shoulders and waved it off. George and Charlie followed Mark into the shop.

"Go ahead Mark, look around," said Charlie, as he watched Mark head towards the back of the store. Mark didn't look at any other items on the way. Reaching the back wall and with a trembling hand, he pointed to the coat hanger.

"How did you know about the coat hanger? That's been a family secret for years" asked Charlie as he stared at Mark.

"It was in my dream." Mark explained, "along with the glass case, the projector and the spiral staircase leading to the special room, what about that quill pen?"

Charlie looked at George. "I don't know how or what, but I believe Mark has been picked to be the next owner. It could be the necklace he wears. Remember, it too came from the 'room'."

Mark was still overwhelmed with what had transpired. As soon as he could, he would move to Rossville to fulfill his destiny.

Would he discover new and more items that were not in his dream? Would they be real with powers beyond imagination? Or was this really just a dream?

THE WEB

My name is Ralph. I have been retired for about five years. I enjoy going over and visiting my neighbors. My wife passed away seven years ago, so I just visit with people and work in my garden and yard to keep my mind occupied. This story is just too much for the old mind to believe. May I ask before I begin? Do you like spiders and are you afraid of them? Think about it before you continue.

I remember that summer, seven years ago, very well. It was so hot and we hadn't received any rain for about five weeks. There was an abundance of bumble bees, mosquitoes, wasps and spiders. Oh *yes,* those spiders! A person couldn't take a step for all those sticky webs filled with crickets, moths and grasshoppers. Yep, I remember that year, very well; very well indeed. In fact, that was the year ole Sidney Rogers and his wife Carol met their demise. There was no sign of foul play or anything like that. It is still an unsolved mystery. To everyone...except me.

Yes sir, it seems like it happened just the other day. I can even remember when I first met Sidney down at the hardware store. About six months prior to Rogers' disappearance, we had become good friends. The last week before Sidney disappeared, he was in the same store and was complaining about spiders all over his tomato plants. He said he was going to get rid of the damn things once and for all. I tried to explain to him that they would help keep the bugs down, but he wouldn't listen.

Sidney once told me that he had been afraid of spiders ever since he was a little kid, where he had walked face first into a web full of dead bugs. It was enough trauma with the bugs; but then the spider started across the web heading for his face, that did it. By the time he got out of the web, he was trembling with fear.

Being my neighbor, I went over to his place later that evening and took him some watermelons and cantaloupe from my garden. When I got there, Sidney was out in the garden and Carol was in the kitchen fixing dinner. I didn't want to stay, so I laid the melons on the counter and told Carol I'd be back in a day or two, to bring them some more. I had a bountiful crop and wanted to share. She thanked me and bid me farewell.

As I was walking out, Sidney met me at the door. He was white as a sheet, muttering loudly about something. I asked what was wrong: and he told us he had run across the biggest spider he had ever seen when he was in the garden watering the tomatoes. After getting him calmed down, we had him retell his story about the spider. Carol and I both knew that Sidney always had a phobia about spiders so we just humored him, and then I went on home.

A couple of days later, I drove over to the Rogers' house to deliver some more melons and see if they would like to come over that evening and have some grilled burgers with me. As I pulled in the drive, I noticed both their vehicles were in the drive and figured they were home. I typically didn't call first; I just went over.

As I was parking the truck, I saw the side door standing wide open. Thinking that was kind of odd, I cautiously went up to the house. As I reached the open door, I called out for them. Getting no reply, I Figured they might be out back in the garden. So, I closed the door and went in search of Carol and Sidney.

As I approached the back yard, you know what I found? Not Sidney, nor his wife, but the biggest spider web I had ever seen in my life. I had to check it out. It was taller than me and I am 6 ft 2. The right top mooring thread, which appeared to be the size of one of my electrical cords, was anchored to one of the fruit trees on the far edge of their garden. The left top mooring thread was anchored to another tree further down the garden. The inside threads going to the center hub were about half that size. Lastly, there was a dewy looking substance dripping from each thread on the web.

Looking around for something to probe the web, I found a stick pile they had been building up for a nice fire. So, I went over and grabbed a meaty, long stick. Walking back over to the web, I poked at it. The web was very sticky and I could hardly remove the stick from it once it made contact.

All of the sudden, hundreds of tiny spiders came to the disturbance where I had poked the web. Now this made me shiver and made my fear of spiders increase quite a bit. After all, a web about six feet square and appearing like a blanket hanging on a clothesline to dry, would frighten just about anyone.

I started searching again for Carol and Sidney. I looked all around outside the house. I searched the out buildings and found nothing. Finally, I went back inside the house to double check that no one had come in while I was outside searching. The door being open led me to believe that they were not at home. After all, most people shut their doors if they leave or are at home... Heck, all the time.

Maybe someone tried to rob them, I thought, I hope they are OK. I couldn't believe that someone would try to hurt them. They were the friendliest people in our town. Both were retired and just stayed around the house enjoying the quiet. They only went to the store if need be.

Circling around again, I was now back at the edge of the garden behind Roger's house. This time I took a better look at the big web. As I got closer, I noticed it was really full of hundreds of baby spiders. A shiver went down my spine as I saw them scurry across and then down the web and head in my direction. As I backed away from it, not seeing the branch on the ground behind me. I tripped and fell. Scrambling to get up, I felt something touch my leg.

As I looked down, I saw the biggest spider I had ever seen. It was about the same diameter as a softball, with two little beady eyes. It crawled onto my foot and started to move up my leg. Slowly reaching down, I gripped my stick from earlier and swung it at the spider. I guess it knew what I was trying to do. It moved to the side like lightning, it avoided the stick and then sank its fangs into my shin.

The pain was the worst I had ever experienced. Before I could swing the stick again and make contact with the spider's body, the fangs sank deeper. Swinging again I finally made contact; the spider flew through the air about twenty feet away. I grabbed my aching leg and tried to get my wits about me.

The spider sat there for a second or two and then started to approach me again. I used the stick to help me get back on my feet to face the spider. Awkwardly, I swung the stick once again and caught the side of the spider with enough force that flipped it through the air again. I could have sworn it screamed as it flew through the air. This time, landing on its back.

I knew this was my chance to strike it again with the stick. Approaching the spider, I raised my makeshift weapon above my head. The spider was still on its back, kicking its legs, sort of trying to re-right itself. I brought the sharp end down; it went deep inside the belly of the spider. I left it there, in the body, where I had stabbed it. I stepped back and watched it squirm.

I thought it was over. Then all of a sudden, hundreds of baby spiders came scrambling over and covered the big one that I just killed. Within moments there was no trace of it. As I watched; I saw a few were headed towards me. I turned to get away, but as I turned to leave, I tripped again. I landed about a foot away from the web. I reached out grasping for something to break my fall. One arm touched the spider's web and the other arm smacked a sharp rock.

As I tried jerking away from the web with no success, I noticed that luckily it was the sleeve of my shirt that was stuck to the web and not my arm. Squirming around I finally pulled my arm out of the long sleeve of my shirt. As I did, I saw little spiders come from everywhere; down the web, from the tomatoes, cucumber patch, stalks of corn, even the strawberries and they covered the shirt. As I scrambled up again, I saw blood oozing from my forearm. Apparently, the rock had done a number on my arm, it was already turning black and blue with a deep scrape in the middle poking through the skin. I thought to myself: 'If I get out of here, that's going to leave a mark".

I started to turn to get away and as I did, my attention was drawn to the other side of the garden about thirty feet away. The scenery didn't match the rest of the garden. Even though I needed to get away from the spiders, I worked my way around the other side to get a better look. As I reached the the radishes, I saw there were two skeletons clean as a whistle.

The skeletons were in a position that looked like they might be trying to crawl away from someone, or something. Maybe one was trying to help the other escape whatever horror that killed them. I didn't know who it was or they might have been. But I had a good idea who it might be by the size. Also I had an idea what caused it. Since neither of Rogers's were roaming around, I figured it might be Carol and Sidney.

Turning around and limp skipping out of the radishes... boy they look tasty, I finally got out of the garden area. I went back into the house to use Sydney's phone to call the sheriff's office. As I told the dispatcher what I had found, I was starting to get a little light headed so I told her that as well.

After I hung up the phone, I really needed to sit down so I went back to my car to wait. It wasn't long till a couple of police cars and an ambulance arrived. They asked me several questions. Was I hurt? Was anyone else involved? Where were the bones? How did you get hurt? I answered the best I could, but I was still a little weak from the fray with the spiders. The Sheriff told me they would be in touch if they needed anything else. I could tell he didn't believe me.

As the EMTs had a hell of a time trying to get me to lie down on the gurney. I had another light headed spell and almost fell backwards off the gurney. After finally getting me laid down and buckled in, then they lifted it up and slid me inside the ambulance. Closing the doors, they drove to the hospital. No sirens, just lights, I wasn't dying. Shortly thereafter, I arrived at the emergency room. Thankfully it was practically void of patients and I didn't have to wait long to see a physician.

"Could you tell me how you got your injuries?" asked the doctor.

"I tripped over a limb and fell. As I went down, my body kind of twisted sideways and my arm hit a sharp rock." Thinking the whole time, they wouldn't believe the part about the spiders, so I kept that to myself for now.

"Do you have any more injuries? If not, we will get your arm x-rayed. I am sure it's not broken but just as precaution," said the doctor as he started to walk away.

"There is one more thing," I said as I raised my jeans to expose my shin.

The ER doctor stopped and returned to the bedside. "Hmmm? That looks like a spider bite. It would have to have been a very large spider though," he said as he ordered the nurse to give me a shot of antibiotics. With that, the doctor left the room.

After getting some bandages on the wounds, a shot, and a couple of x-rays of my arm, they released me to go home and make an appointment with my regular physician. I called a taxi and went to Rogers to get my car and go home, hoping to relax.

A few hours later I was sitting in my recliner trying to take a nap, the sheriff called, waking me from a troubled sleep and asked me if I would come back over to the Rogers' residence. Taking a survey of my old body and freshly bandaged wounds, noticing the new aches and pains that needed a couple weeks to heal. I asked the sheriff when, and he said now. Figuring I could drive, I wasn't in such bad shape as to tell him no, I relented and said I would be over in a jiffy.

I arrived at Sydney's within a few minutes and the sheriff, George Thornton, was standing there holding the incident report in his hand.

"Didn't you say something about spiders and webs?" he asked. I repeated once again what I had seen.

"Well, come out here to the back of the house by the garden," said the sheriff as he led the way.

"We have removed the bones and are sending them to the Medical Examiner. We can assume those were human bones. We will know for sure when the M. E. gets done with them. Just can't figure out what happened to the Roger's, though. I know what you told me, but look," said the sheriff as he motioned to the garden site.

As I stared at the trees where the web had been, I noticed that there were no spiders, no web, nothing as I remembered it. There were no bugs crawling or flying about. Even though the large web was gone. As Sheriff Thornton got into his patrol car, he turned to me and said he'd be in touch.

A few days later the Sheriff contacted me, again. "They got the results of the dental records that proved that it was Carol and Sidney's remains that were found by the garden," Sheriff Thornton said as he shook his head in disbelief.

"This case is going to take some time. Like I said, I may need to talk to you again," he said with an uncertain tone in his voice.

"Sure," I replied. "You have my phone number. Just give me a call."

I decided to look once again for any of the spiders. I went out back to the garden and I knelt down on one knee and looked at the plants in the garden. There were bugs and worms and all kinds of little critters, except no spiders. Not even a web, like before. Where had they gone?

Now, may I ask. Do you have a garden? Or maybe a small timber at the back edge of your yard? Seen any bugs around the garden or birds setting in the trees?

Maybe the spiders came to visit you! Look very carefully!!

Oh, don't forget, they do like closets and under beds!

Hole 13

The Ford pickup rattled along the gravel road, its tires kicking up a cloud of dust that swirled around the vehicle like a choking veil. The sun, now hanging low in the sky, cast long, unforgiving beams that illuminated the worn-out truck's battered exterior.

The once-pristine paint was now peeling and faded, a silent testament to years of neglect, exposure to the elements, and countless miles of dirt roads. The truck groaned with every bump in the road, the frame straining under the weight of both age and the harsh journey it had endured. Tom gripped the steering wheel tighter, the worn leather of the wheel slick against his calloused palms. He could feel the weariness creeping into his bones, the weight of the miles pressing down on him with each passing minute.

Inside the cab, the air was thick with the smell of dust, oil, and stale leather. Tom tightened a handkerchief around his face, hoping it would shield him from the grit that slipped through the rust-eaten holes in the floorboards. But the cloth barely offered any protection. He could feel the dry particles settling on his skin, coating him like a second layer. His throat itched, his eyes stung, and the constant hum of the engine seemed to mock him, a reminder of just how far he had traveled—both physically and emotionally.

The truck's engine sputtered once more, the coughing sound echoing in the still air. Tom gritted his teeth, his eyes narrowing in frustration. It wasn't just the engine that was starting to give out. It was everything—the truck, the road, and the endless journey ahead of him. He wasn't a man who typically sought stability or permanence, but something about the relentless grind of life on the road had begun to wear him down.

The open road, once a symbol of freedom and escape, had started to feel like a prison. He had been drifting for years, never staying in one place for too long, never forming connections that might tie him to any one spot. It was a life of isolation, a life where the road was both his escape and his trap.

But now, he was nearing the end of yet another chapter. The destination this time was a place called Hole Thirteen, a remote oil drilling site that had earned a reputation for being... different. People talked about it in whispers, their voices dropping to a murmur whenever it came up. There was something about the place, something unsettling, as if the land itself held secrets that should remain buried. The name alone—Hole Thirteen—was enough to spark rumors and fuel superstitions.

Tom wasn't one to believe in such things. He had seen too much of the world, too much of the grime and grit that came with the rougher edges of life, to give any credence to stories about curses or restless spirits. Still, as he drew closer to the site, something about the whole situation gnawed at him. He couldn't quite shake the feeling that he was stepping into something much darker than he was prepared for.

The truck's engine gave one final cough, and then sputtered into a reluctant silence. Tom leaned forward, his brow furrowed in concentration, and gave the dashboard a reassuring pat. "Come on, old girl, just a little further," he muttered, more to himself than to the truck. His words were an attempt at comfort, a way of calming his nerves, but they felt hollow.

The landscape stretched out in front of him, barren and unforgiving, the ground cracked and dry as if the land itself was starved of life. The occasional scrub brush dotted the earth, their spindly branches twisted and gnarled, struggling to survive in the harsh environment. The horizon shimmered with the heat, making everything appear as though it were floating just out of reach. There was nothing here, nothing that could offer solace or a sense of purpose. Just empty space, stretching on forever.

Tom was used to the desolation. His life mirrored the land in many ways. He drifted from job to job, never staying in one place for too long, never planting roots. It was a life of freedom, yes, but also one of solitude and emptiness. Each job was just another stop along the way, each new town just another place to fill the void before he moved on again.

The promise of work at Hole Thirteen hadn't seemed any different from the others at first. An oil rig in a forgotten corner of the world, offering a paycheck and a few weeks of hard labor. But the rumors, the whispers of something not quite right about the place, had followed him even as he crossed the state line.

The foreman had assured him that the job itself would be simple, that no special skills or experience were needed. But there was something about the name, something about the timing—Friday the thirteenth—that made the air feel thick with tension. Tom was no superstitious man, but even he couldn't deny that the odds were starting to stack up against him.

When the rig site finally came into view, Tom felt a small surge of relief. The trucks parked in uneven rows, engines rumbling and whining, gave the place a sense of life, of activity. The workers moved about, their voices rising above the din of machinery, their faces weathered and worn from long days under the sun. The towering derricks stood in the distance, their skeletal frames looming like silent sentinels. The sun cast long shadows across the dusty ground, stretching out toward the horizon, as if the entire world was holding its breath.

Tom parked the truck at the edge of the site, its brakes protesting with a high-pitched screech as it came to a halt. Dust clung to his boots and jeans as he stepped out of the cab, the familiar weight of the workday settling over him like a second skin. The heat hit him in a wave, but it was the stifling silence that made his skin crawl. It was as if the land itself was holding its breath, waiting for something to happen.

A few men approached him, offering curt nods and firm handshakes. They were the kind of men who had lived hard lives—sun-scorched faces, hands calloused from years of labor. There was an unease in their eyes, something that wasn't immediately apparent but that lingered beneath the surface.

One man, shorter than the rest, made a joke about the site's infamous reputation. "Hope you're not one of those superstitious types," he said with a grin, but there was an edge to his voice that didn't quite match the levity of his words. Another man, with a thick beard and a weathered expression, chuckled and added, "Thirteen's not just a number around here; it's a whole mood."

Tom smiled politely, but the unease that hung in the air was undeniable. The men's words were laced with humor, but there was something about the way they spoke that made it clear they weren't joking. They were afraid. Tom didn't know why, but he felt it. The hair on the back of his neck stood on end, and the weight of the land seemed to press in on him from all sides. It wasn't just the remote location or the hard labor that made the place unsettling—it was something more, something older, something that had been here long before the drilling rigs and the men who worked them.

John, a wiry man with a quick smile and a mischievous glint in his eye, clapped Tom on the shoulder. "You'll get used to it," he said, his tone light, but there was something in his eyes that gave Tom pause. "Just don't look over your shoulder too much. Folks say something's always watching out here."

Tom chuckled and nodded, brushing off the comment. But even as he did, he felt the weight of those words settle into the pit of his stomach. There was a chill in the air, a sense that the place was alive in ways he didn't understand. It was as if the land had a pulse, a heartbeat that was out of sync with everything else.

The foreman's voice cut through the murmur of conversation, calling everyone to attention. The men gathered around as the foreman pinned a notice to the weathered bulletin board. His voice was strong and commanding, carrying the authority of a man who had spent years in the field, barking orders and managing the chaos of a drilling site. "Listen up," he said, his tone leaving little room for argument. "Ross Oil has settled its dispute with the local tribes. The courts ruled in our favor. We're clear to drill."

A ripple of murmurs spread through the crowd. Tom caught snippets of conversation—talk of burial grounds and ancestral lands, of a history that ran deep beneath the earth. The foreman raised his hand to quiet the group, his expression hardening. "Starting tonight, we're implementing guard shifts," he continued. "Two men per shift until we have a permanent system in place. You'll get time-and-a-half pay and the following day off. Volunteers?"

The foreman's voice cut through the murmur of the crowd, its sharp edge silencing the men who had gathered around the bulletin board. They turned their attention to him as he stepped forward, his boots crunching on the dry ground, the familiar crackle of paper echoing. He was a seasoned veteran, someone who had worked through the worst that the oil fields could throw at him. His voice carried the authority of a man who had spent years managing the chaos of noisy rigs, barking orders through the hum of machinery and the dust of the desert.

There were whispers of the land being cursed, of spirits angered by the intrusion of drilling rigs on land that had been sacred long before the first pipeline was laid. Some of the workers looked uneasy, their faces tight as they exchanged wary glances. But the foreman silenced them with a raised hand, his face hardening as he continued.

The silence that followed was thick with tension. Tom could feel the weight of the moment pressing down on him, the strange heaviness in the air that seemed to hold its breath. Men shifted uneasily from foot to foot, casting furtive glances at each other. No one moved. No one volunteered.

Tom could see the hesitation in their eyes. There was fear, yes, but something deeper—something primal. These men had seen their fair share of rough days, weathered countless storms and faced danger in ways that would have broken weaker men. But this was different. There was something about the place that made their bodies go stiff, made their words falter. It wasn't the usual grumble of hard work or the threat of an oil spill or equipment failure. No, it was something intangible, a sense that the land itself was fighting back, resisting the intrusion of men and machines.

When no one stepped forward, the foreman sighed deeply, his shoulders slumping under the weight of responsibility. He pulled his hat off his head, running a hand through his graying hair. Then, he reached into his jacket pocket and pulled out a stack of slips of paper.

He began to call names. One by one, the men reluctantly stepped forward. Each name seemed to hang in the air a little longer than the last, as though the site itself was drawing the moments out, waiting for something inevitable.

"Tom," the foreman said at last, his gaze finding Tom in the crowd. "Looks like you're up for the thirteenth."

The air seemed to shift then, the collective breath of the men in the group held in uneasy anticipation. The foreman's voice softened, his expression shifting to one of sympathy. "Sorry, Tom. It's just the way it worked out."

Tom nodded, swallowing the lump in his throat. There was nothing he could say. It wasn't as if he could refuse the assignment. He didn't have the luxury of choice—not with bills to pay, no savings to fall back on, and the unrelenting pressure of keeping his head above water. The land stretched out in front of him, a barren wasteland of dust and scrub, but now it felt like the whole world was closing in. He wanted to refuse, to get in the truck and drive as far away from this cursed place as he could. But there was nowhere to go. The oil field was his next paycheck, the next step in his never-ending search for work. So, he accepted it with a nod, trying to convince himself that it was just another job—nothing more.

As the sun sank below the horizon, casting the desert in shadows, the site transformed. The dust seemed to grow thicker, more oppressive, as the last vestiges of daylight faded. The workers scattered, returning to their trailers or gathering around the fire pits, leaving the site silent and still. The hum of machinery was replaced by an eerie stillness, the kind of silence that only deepens as night falls. Tom settled near the base of the rig, a lantern flickering weakly at his side. Its feeble light fought against the darkness, casting long shadows on the ground, each one shifting as if alive.

Tom pulled out his paperback, *Diary of Death*. The title seemed grimly appropriate for the mood that had settled over the site. He turned to the first page, but the words blurred in front of his eyes. His mind kept drifting back to the events of the day—the strange sense of unease, the foreman's grim tone, the hushed whispers that followed him everywhere he went. He tried to push it out of his mind, but it gnawed at him, eating away at his concentration. That was when he felt it—a low, rumbling tremor beneath his feet. At first, it was so faint that he questioned whether it was real. Perhaps it was just the wind, or the rig shifting in the ground. But then the ground trembled again, more pronounced this time, enough to make the lantern flicker.

His heart skipped a beat. The low rumble grew louder, vibrating through the soles of his boots. Tom froze, his hand instinctively reaching for the two-way radio clipped to his belt. He pressed the button, his voice trembling as he spoke. "Base, this is Hole Thirteen. Do you copy?"

Static crackled in response, a low hiss followed by bursts of garbled sound. He strained his ears, listening for any sign of a reply, but all he heard was the relentless buzzing of static. He set the radio down, his unease growing with each passing second. He glanced around the darkened site, the shadows of the derricks stretching long across the ground, their skeletal frames rising from the earth like ancient giants.

Then, the rumble came again. Stronger. Closer. Tom's breath caught in his throat. The ground beneath him shuddered as though something massive was moving below, something that could not be ignored. He looked toward the base of the derrick, his eyes narrowing against the growing darkness. That was when he saw it. A faint glow, barely perceptible at first, began to emerge from the ground. It spread slowly, pulsing with a rhythmic intensity that seemed to match the beat of his racing heart. The glow grew brighter, expanding outward, filling the space around him with an unnatural light.

Tom stood frozen, his heart pounding in his chest. He could feel the heat radiating from the glow, even from a distance, and he was unable to tear his eyes away from the bizarre sight. The light seemed to shift, a swirling mass that began to take shape—something was emerging from it. The air grew thick with the scent of burning wood, and the temperature around him spiked, making the sweat on his skin feel like fire.

The figure that emerged from the light was unlike anything Tom had ever seen. It was humanoid, yes, but its features were sharp, its skin glowing with a faint, otherworldly light. The figure was dressed in traditional Native American garb, its body adorned with feathers, beads, and intricate patterns. In one hand, it held a gleaming hatchet, its blade catching the light in a way that seemed to make it shimmer with unnatural fire. Its eyes burned with an intensity that struck Tom to his very core. They were not human eyes. They were ancient, eternal eyes—eyes that had seen centuries pass and had borne witness to unspeakable things.

Tom's body locked in place. Every instinct screamed at him to run, to get as far away from this terrifying apparition as possible. But his legs wouldn't move. His breath caught in his throat, his heart hammering in his chest as he stared into the figure's glowing gaze.

"White man," the voice boomed, deep and resonant, carrying the weight of ages. "What gives you the right to disturb our sacred ground? For your trespass, I claim your soul."

The words reverberated through him, shaking his very foundation. His pulse raced, his mind struggling to make sense of what was happening. Every part of him wanted to scream, to flee, but his body refused to obey. He could feel the heat from the flames drawing closer, tendrils of fire licking the air around him. They stretched toward him, reaching with an unnatural speed, burning with an intensity that seemed to scorch his very soul.

Then the world exploded into darkness.
The next morning, the workers discovered Tom's lifeless body near the rig, his face frozen in a contorted expression of terror. His eyes were wide open, staring

blankly at the sky. The coroner's report concluded that he had suffered a heart attack, a natural cause of death.

But among the crew, the whispers told a different story. "Something scared him to death," one man murmured, his voice tight with fear. Others nodded; their eyes shadowed with unease.

Another guard, a man who had volunteered for the next shift, was found hanging from the rig's framework. His throat had been slit, the body hanging like a twisted marionette. A third victim came soon after—the foreman himself, his throat slashed under inexplicable circumstances. The authorities struggled to explain it, their investigations yielding only confusion and fear. The site was abandoned shortly after. No one was willing to return after the strange incident.

The company made a decisive move, closing the site for good. The rigs were dismantled, the land was left untouched, and Hole Thirteen was sealed. The whispers, however, never ceased. Locals still speak of the place in hushed tones, of flickering lights in the distance and disembodied voices carried on the wind. On Friday the thirteenth, the air grows thick with a palpable tension, and the land seems to hold its breath. The curse of Hole Thirteen endures, a chilling reminder of what happens when man disturbs what was never meant to be touched.

To this day, no one dares approach Hole Thirteen, particularly after dark or on Friday the thirteenth.

Although the site is capped and abandoned, locals believe the spirits of the land continue to watch over it, haunting the area especially on Friday the thirteenth.

    Job opportunity: A guard is needed to oversee Hole Thirteen. Inquire within.

Well-Seasoned

Bill Davis was nineteen years old. He was waiting for fall to get here so he could start his first year of college. Randy liked to party and also liked to consume his portion of the alcoholic beverages. This party was no different. His friends tried to get him to slow down. That seemed to be a waste of breath. "I'm fine. Don't you worry about me, I can handle this and a lot more," he said as he gulped another beer.

"At least let one of us drive you, home. You are in no shape to get behind the wheel," begged his close friend George.

"Alright, alright, I will come get you when I'm ready to leave," replied Bill, as he lifted another beer to his lips.

"Ok, I'm counting on that," said George as he headed for the bathroom.

"Good. Now is a good time to leave. I will show them," mumbled Bill. He staggered, wobbled, and tripped a few times, finally reaching his car. Dropping his keys on the ground and putting his right index finger to his lips he made the "shhhh" sound. Of course, no one was there to hear the keys hit the cement. Bill grabbed the door handle, pulled the door open and got in. He sat in the front seat of his 1999 Ford Mustang and tried three times to put the key in the ignition. Finally, hitting the hole and inserting the key, he gave it a twist. The cylinders responded. On the second try, Bill managed to grab the shifter and pulled the shift stick into drive.

The Wreck

Bill headed down the street. He thought he would take the freeway to save time to get back home. He still lived at home with his parents. Bill had thought he would wait to go to college and live in the dorm. He turned the corner making a wide turn into the opposite lane. Luckily no one was in the other lane. After he got the car aligned back up within the lane and headed down the street, he accelerated as he headed up the on ramp. He was getting ready to merge into the traffic, but Bill didn't look up soon enough.

As he entered the freeway lane he felt the steering jerk in his hands. He had hit something or someone. He didn't know which, but it was too late to get out of the way. The eight back wheels of the semi he had pulled under came over top of him. He sobered up, but it was too late. The metal roof smashed and twisted down on him. His body resembled that of a butcher's meat grinder churning out hamburger. Blood splattered everywhere. His limbs were smashed from his body. And finally, his head popped like a giant pimple.

The semi came to a screeching halt after the rear wheels made contact with the pavement again. The Mustang was unrecognizable. One tangled mess with blood all over it and the pavement. One wouldn't think there was that much blood in the human body, but being mangled and flattened that much, makes one wonder.

When the police arrived, they looked the situation over and after finding Bill's body, or what was left of it, called the coroner. An ambulance would have been useless for the boy, but the driver of the semi might need some attention. There was no "body" to resuscitate.

The Clean Up

Tom Biggs was the corner, medical examiner, and mortician. He arrived at the scene in his Ford van. Opening the back doors of the van, which was identified by the word Corner painted across the back. Reaching in, Tom pulled out a bag. It was about the size of an Army duffle bag. It contained the tools of his trade.

Walking over to one of the policemen, he had to dodge several pieces of the Mustang. Once he reached them, he could see the blood and body parts scattered everywhere.

"Well," started Tom. "I can tell you step one is definite. He is dead."

"Second," he continued. "I could use some to help me find all the body parts. At least as much as we can. Boy, the car's metal sliced him up pretty good."

Just then an ambulance pulled up, with lights flashing.

"Better check out the driver of the truck. The one in the car is gone." said Tom

Deputy Larry Rauls, was assigned to help Tom pick up the pieces. He had been on the force about two years and had never seen anything like this before. Tom and Larry put on masks and gloves. Tom had pulled a gurney with a body bag laying on it over to the car, what was left of it.

Tom noticed that on the other side of the wreck was a dog licking up some blood and then tearing at some of the parts, like it was fresh steak thrown to him. He waved his arms in the air and yelled, trying to scare the dog off. The German Shepherd started to bolt but quickly turned and grabbed a piece of the body, then took off.

Tom reached into his bag and took out two putty knives and two pairs of vinyl gloves. He handed one to Larry and pointed to the mess ahead of them.

"I want to try and put what parts we get back in order they go. If you don't know, ask," said Tom as he bent down to pick up one of the kid's arms.

Tom and Larry were scraping body parts from the car, from the pavement, and even some from the truck's tires. It was a tedious job and took them about three hours.

Upon returning to the morgue, Tom called the local dentist and told them he needed dental records for positive identification. He told them who the police and himself thought the victim could be.

They brought the records over within half an hour. Almost immediately Tom called the Police and told them their guess was right. It was Bill Davis. On this verification, they called and informed his parents. They then called Tom to see if they could see their son. Tom hated this part of the job, especially in these cases.

"Could I speak with you first?" asked Tom to the mother.

"I want to see my son!" she replied back, in a very demanding voice.

"May I come to your house first?" Tom asked.

She dropped the phone as tears streamed down her cheeks.

"What is the problem?" asked the father in a choked-up voice.

"I need to talk to you in person," answered Tom.

"Ok, we'll be right over." said Ralph, Bill's father. He was a big man but he was on the verge of crying. After all, it was his son.

"You don't..." the conversation was over. Tom was going to tell them he would come to their house.

Sue was the first to enter the coroner's office. "Ok where is he?" she asked.

"Please let me talk to the both of you first." pleaded Tom.

"Ok, go ahead," stated Ralph.

Tom explained about the wreck, the truck, spending around three hours trying to put Bill back to some sort of order. Then he told them they had to get dental records to verify him.

"I'm sorry but I believe you should have the body cremated as soon as possible and not have even a closed casket. Just set out pictures and remember him that way."

After carefully considering what Tom had told them, they decided that he was right and gave him the ok to proceed.

Business Problems

Terri was Tom Biggs' younger sister. She was a brunette and was about five eight. She wasn't married but she ran the local cafe, the Cup and Saucer, by herself and one waitress. Almost every business day's end she would go by Tom's place and have a nightcap. His home was above the funeral business.

Today was no different. It was 10:30 pm and she needed that nightcap real bad tonight.

"Tom," started Terri. "I went over the books for the restaurant and it doesn't look good. I didn't make enough last week to pay for the meat delivery. I had to dip into my savings. There isn't a whole lot there. I can't keep going on this way. I'm thinking about closing the doors,"

"Now hang on. Let me see what I can do." said Tom, giving his sister a hug.

Tom didn't have a clue on what to do. He knew how much his sister loved the restaurant and the town they were in. They sat together batting ideas back and forth.

After about an hour and several sighs later. Terri gave her brother a hug and said goodnight. Tom was rubbing his chin as he closed the door.

He jerked the door open and yelled for Terri to come back.

"What?" she asked as she entered the doorway.

"Follow me," said Tom. They headed towards the back room.

"I don't want to go back to your work room as you call it," said Terri as she stopped in her tracks.

"Fine, let me go first and make sure everything is cleaned up," said Tom

Tom did find a few pieces of Bill laying on the edge of the table. He scraped them up and placed them in a stainless-steel pan and placed it in his fridge he used for his personal use. He then wiped up any excess blood and headed out to the front of his building to tell Terri to come to the back.

"I have an idea. I'm going to make a pot of chili tonight and if it turns out good enough. Then I think we might have a solution to your problem," said Tom with confidence.

"I don't understand how this will help my financial situation," said Terri with skepticism.

"You let me worry about that," added Tom.

"Do you have all the stuff you need?"

"Oh, no problem. I have the meat in my fridge and the seasonings in my cupboard."

Terri said goodbye once again, only this time she really left, shaking her head in disbelief.

The Recipe

Tom immediately put a large pot on his stove and went to the fridge and got out the meat. He tore it up in small pieces and put the fire on low. He wanted it to simmer slowly and let the meat flavor soak into the beans.

He stirred the chili and took a sip. "Yuck, it has a taste of a little seasoning from the beans, but not enough."

He looked in the cupboard for some chili seasoning. His bottle was empty.

Tom turned and looked at the bottle in the corner of the room on the shelf. The label read," Well Seasoned". Tom never did understand what the label meant. He took the gallon glass jar over to the table. After he opened the lid, he smelled the contents.

"Wow," said Tom. "It smells like chili, unbelievable."

"I bought this at an oddities shop in another town. I believe the owner's name was Mark He did tell me that the things in the lower floor had special powers. Well, I don't see any kind of power, just a seasoning. I will start with a couple tablespoons and see what that does to it," said Mark aloud.

After stirring the seasoning in the meat and beans, Tom tasted the brew.

"Oh man! This taste is unreal. I have never tasted chili this good," replied Tom out loud.
"I got to call Terri back and have her come over for a taste," said Tom as he picked up the phone.

"Terri, come over, right now. I think I found something to help you out," said Tom sipping another taste,

Terri left and headed over to her brother's place. It was a short drive and arrived within fifteen minutes.

"Ok, what idea did you come up with?" asked Terri

"Taste this chili," said Tom, handing her a bowl.

Terri took a spoon full and put it in her mouth.
"Wow, that is good! "

"Yes. If we made this at the restaurant, I think it would go over very well," added Tom. "What do you think?"

"Sounds good. How did you make it?" asked Terri, refilling her bowl.

"I took the meat out of my fridge and simmered it, added the beans and then the seasoning."

"Meat out of the fridge? Didn't you have a victim of a wreck today? You didn't. Oh God, tell me you didn't," stated Terri in a nervous tone.

"Well... of course not. It's the seasoning. I used the two pounds of hamburger I had bought at the store. I'm crazy, but not stupid," answered Tom with a chuckle.

The Well

"Let me explain. About a month ago I went through this small town and stopped at an antique shop. Whatever you want to call it. I decided to stop and look around. The owner's name was Mark. I looked at several items, then he came over and asked if there was anything in particular I was looking for. I told him I liked things out of the ordinary. He motioned for me to follow him to the rear of the room and down a spiral staircase. Mark told me things down there were special," said Tom as he took ahold of his sister's hands as if to lead her.

"Right there," added Tom pointing to the jar.

"What's that mean, 'on the side'?" asked Terri.

"You won't believe me, unless I show you," said Tom, letting go of her hands and grabbing the jar. He removed the lid and reached in with a clean cup he pulled out a cup full and watched as the powder replenished itself. He poured it back and it stayed the same level.

"See what I mean?" asked Tom. "You can make that great tasting chili with this seasoning and never run out."

"I think I understand 'Well Seasoned'. It means a well of seasoning and never runs out," added Terri.

"I wonder if it works on other things? Like steak and roast and maybe chops?" asked Terri as she stuck her finger in the jar and tasted it once again.

"I have one thought, rather a question. I wonder what it's made of and where it came from. Do you think there could be any "side effects"? added Tom.

"Well, that will probably have to be determined later," said Terri.

"What do you mean?" asked Tom.

"Let's make a batch of chili at the restaurant. Then we'll see if anything happens." replied Terri.

"What if someone dies?" asked Tom.

"Then we'll know the recipe wasn't any good," replied Terri with a snicker.

"Yeah right, then we will be……." Tom started.

"Wait, we can make a batch and see if it bothers us," interrupted Terri.

"Ok, let's do it!" said Tom.

Two months later

Things were going pretty well for both Tom and Terri. The restaurant business was doing great for Terri. No one was having any side effects from the chili and Terri decided to make it and sell it in the restaurant. People loved it and it sold almost as fast as they made it and the seasoning never ran out.

Terri started sprinkling a little in the burgers and then some on the steaks. The restaurant was doing so well that Terri had to hire extra help.

Tom's business was as usual. Nothing had changed for him.

Then two months went by and things started going downhill fast. People that came into the restaurant started to get gray hair and complained about their aches and pains. Some women were complaining about getting crow's feet too early. They too complained about aches and pains. The children were looking older than they should. There was one exception. One child about nine years old didn't like chili so he didn't eat it. Terri remembered him. He only wanted hotdogs, which Terri didn't season.

That night Terri called her brother. "We may have a problem," she said on the phone.

"And what that might be?" asked Tom.

"I've been having a lot of extra pain. Legs, back, my feet, and even my fingers." answered Terri with a worried tone in her voice.

"Oh, you're just getting old," said Tom with a chuckle.

"That's the point. I think that seasoning does have a side effect. It speeds up the aging process." said Terri

Terri explained to Tom about the father with graying hair, the wife looking in a compact mirror and complaining about lines at her age. The young boy looked normal like he had every time they came into eat, no signs of any effects. Of course he had hotdogs. No seasoning there.

"We can't call anyone. There hasn't been a crime, yet," said Tom as he talked to Terri.

Tom knew if that continued the people would die before their time. He decided to go over to his sister's place after she closed and talk to her.

Tom held his sister's hands across her kitchen table. He looked her straight in the eyes and started to tell her his idea.

"Look, we don't know for sure if the seasoning is speeding up the aging process or not.
If they do age faster, then my business picks up too. You get more customers and evidently so do I," stated Tom with a smile.

"You are gross. Those poor people are not living out their lives to the fullest. You want to make a profit from it?' asked Terri.

"Hey, we didn't commit any crime. You feed them and I put them to rest."

"You do have a point. Ok, but the first time someone starts asking questions, we quit." said Terri as she thought about the profit she had been making.

Then it happened. The figure in the cloak appeared. Walked over to the jar, touched it and the jar and it disappeared. No one knows if it is a ghost or a spirit or just what.

Where do you eat?

Let me ask you. Where do you eat? Is the food exceptionally good to the palate? Are the people extremely nice? Do you feel discomfort after a meal but also satisfied? Well, makes one wonder, doesn't it?

The Drone Rift

Adam Ross had just purchased his new drone. He had crashed several older, cheaper models, practicing the art of flying, until he finally thought he had them figured out. With this confidence he purchased a very expensive drone with a screen that showed him if he was about to crash, and a whole slew of other fancy options. With that particular option, maybe he could avoid those crashes. He could see how close he really was to objects.

He took his new toy and controls out to the open field. After setting everything up, he sent it flying around the field, climbing, diving, curving to the left then to the right, until he felt he was ready. He took it up to about fifty feet and decided to take pictures of his surroundings. At this height the pictures were still very clear. Adam decided to climb to one hundred feet, which was a mistake. There came a loud crack, like the sound of a bolt of lightning. His drone disappeared into thin air. The screen on the controller was still going and what he saw was surreal. Surprisingly, he was still in control of the drone. "What the…I just bought that," yelled Adam.

The scenery was not what one would expect. It showed a town exactly where he was standing, only it wasn't right. It showed buildings, several of them. He knew there had been a small mining town in this area about one hundred years ago. I am confused. I don't know how to bring it back to me.

Adam didn't understand why he still had control of the drone or the images he was getting. He couldn't wait to tell someone, but who would believe such a story. The next decision was made quickly when he moved the stick on the controller. The drone started circling the town and showing the images of the buildings. There were people walking around but their images were transparent, so to speak. Adam thought they looked like ghosts but not quite.

"If I did mention this to anyone, they would have me committed to a padded cell. I need proof," he thought. Then it hit him.

"I pushed the record button on the control when it first took off." He watches the screen as the drone flies around the town. As it was moving about, he noticed there were no shadows: or any reflection on the water as he went over a watering trough. He decided to fly closer to one of the people walking around. As the drone got closer there was no reaction. So, Adam decided to get even closer. Still nothing. "They can't see the drone," he said to himself, as he pulled back on the controller and decided to go explore the town.

The whole town looked like it was just slapped together with bits and pieces of whatever lumber could be found. Getting to the edge of the town Adam saw a sign buried half in the dirt and half out. Hovering above the sign, he made out the letters, "L-A-N-N-O-N"

"Lannon must have been the name of the town, years ago," said Adam as he stared at the sight before him. Then he began to wonder how he was going to recover his drone and all the video it had taken. He made the drone climb to about one hundred feet. He decided to make a three sixty maneuver and look at the surroundings. There was nothing but dirt and sand all the way to the horizon in all directions. Nothing, that is, except the little town below him. Adam had no idea which way he was headed but he just headed straight towards the horizon. He also wondered how the power gauge still showed a full charge.

At that moment there was a loud crack again like before and his drone reappeared. He decided to land immediately and check to see if all that he had seen on his screen had been recorded by the drone.

After Adam looked at the recordings, he looked up the name of the town on his cell phone before he forgot. Lannon, Adam found, was a very small community built right where he was standing, over a hundred years ago..

"Wow, maybe tomorrow I will see if I can return and check out more of the town. That is if I can remember the steps I took to get there and if it will happen again."

LATER THAT EVENING

Not being able to sleep from his discovery, Adam decided to call his friend Maggie Spears. Maggie was about ten years older than Adam and had been good friends for several years. They often confided in each other. As for Maggie, she was what they call an old grump.

"What the hell do you want?' was the answer on the other end of the phone. Adam was not surprised at her tone or words.

"I couldn't sleep. I discovered something and I need to show someone."

"Don't tell me you discovered how to use the phone at… what the hell? it's one-forty in the morning!"

"Sorry, but I was too excited. Can you come over first thing in the morning?"

"Oh, I suppose" was her reply.

With that, Adam hung up and lay there staring at the ceiling in deep thought. He hadn't looked at all of the recordings from the drone yet. He was going to, then decided to wait until tomorrow and share them with Maggie.

The next day came with a lot of questions and disbelief. The recordings were exactly like he had seen on the screen of the controller. The town, the people, and the buildings were just like he had seen previously.

Maggie arrived, with her usual grumpiness.

"What?" This was her greeting to Adam, who was standing in the doorway with the door held open for her. Adam was a man of few possessions, and his furnishings in the house reflected this. His most expensive item was his drone. He had no girlfriend, and not very many friends either. He decided that stuff could come later, especially now after his discoveries.

"Got something I want you to see" replied Adam reaching for his drone, "I recorded this yesterday," he added.

"So... you took a picture, and you had me get up early to see? You crazy, or what?" asked Maggie.

"Take another look. A closer look. Look at the people. See anything unusual?" asked Adam as he pointed to the images in the picture.

"Something wrong with your camera? The images are slightly faded?" stated Maggie as she leaned over and looked at the town and people.

"No, that's what I wanted you to see," said Adam as he began to explain everything.

"Ok, let's find out about another town that was located in a certain area and is no longer there. What do you think?"

"I'm game, but where and how are you going to find another town that is no longer there?" And when are you going to do this? On a weekend?" she asked as she started for the door. She knew Adam worked for the local grocery store and his pay wasn't that great. She knew he was happy there and he had told her someday he would get a better job but he wasn't in any hurry. "The library ought to be a good start," he replied as reached for the door knob for Maggie.

"You'll have to wait till Monday. Today is Saturday and I don't believe they open it on weekends," she answered, stepping through the doorway and outside.

"Call me, and let me know what you find," she yelled back over her shoulder.

The town was too small to afford the library to be open on weekends, so Adam got up early the following Monday. Grabbed a piece of toast and a cup of coffee and headed for the library.

He approached the librarian, Evelyn Banks. She was a retired librarian from Gallery, a nearby city much larger than Wyatt. The town of Wyatt hired Evelyn as librarian at minimum wage. She didn't mind, she just enjoyed books so much. She was very knowledgeable about history.

"Hi Evelyn. May I ask you a question?" asked Adam.

Before she could answer, the door banged open. It was Maggie.

"Sorry, I didn't realize the door was so loose."

"What was your question?" asked Evelyn and smiled at Maggie.

"I'm looking for a town that was within a hundred-mile radius from here that is no longer there. You know, abandoned; like a hundred years or so ago", he asked with a questioning look.

Evelyn looked at Adam. "Well, that is an odd request but I think I might have a location for you", as she headed towards one of the shelves of books. She reached up and pulled down a large book that was in fair condition, probably due to the fact that no one really checked it out that much.

"Be very careful with this book. She said, handing it to him. The binding is old."

"Tell you what." Adam said. "I will let you look it up for me."

"Well, ok. No one else is here right now, so that ought to be okay." "Here it is. The town is called Breeds.

I believe it used to be an old mining town back in the early 1800's."

Adam was getting anxious. "Thanks Evelyn," he said as he carefully picked up the book and looked at the page that showed the town. Slowly turning the pages, Adam turned to Maggie and said,

"Look here. This is it."

Turning back to Evelyn, Adam asked "Would it be okay to take a picture of this town, so I can remember what it looked like?" as he pulled out his cellphone.

"Why do you want her to remember what it looked like?" asked Evelyn.

"Oh, we just compare pictures of what we saw", replied Adam, thinking quickly. He didn't want to try and explain the real reason. He thought "he wasn't lying". They did want to compare pictures to the book and what the drone picked up.

Adam and Maggie headed out the door. He had written down the directions to Breeds and waved them in the air, as he asked Maggie if she wanted to go check it out.

"Hell yes. You got the drone with you?' asked Maggie

"Sure do!" replied Adam.
"Well, let's go!" said Maggie, as she got into the car.

BREEDS

The drive to where Breeds had been located was about an hour and fifteen minutes away. The road went from pavement to gravel. The scenery changed from flat fields of corn and soybeans to trees on both sides of the road. A small stream ran parallel to the road. The dust was rolling up from behind the vehicle and drifting off to the side and into the trees.

Adam noticed that the road was gradually going downward. Realizing that he was in a small valley, and the incline could change suddenly, he slowed down considerably. As he came around the last curve in the road, he saw that he was in a small community. Guessing it was Breeds, he headed on down the road. The houses were all in a line on the north side of the railroad that went through the town. One building looked like it could have been a grocery store many years before. An old one-story school house, which was now someone's home. Adam noticed an old abandoned house on the south side of the tracks.

"Let's park on the road by that old house," said Adam as he headed across the railroad tracks. He pulled over by the old house, leaving the vehicle on the edge of the road. The road was gravel and plenty wide enough for another vehicle to pass.

Getting the drone out, and ready to fly, Adam told Maggie that he had to keep an eye on the monitor to guide the drone to the height he needed.

"How do you know how high you are?" asked Maggie.

"See the numbers on the edge of the screen? That's the height of the drone to the ground" replied Adam.

The gage was showing seventy-eight feet, then ninety feet. Adam slowed down the climb. "Pay attention now, it's close to one hundred feet. That's when the loud crack and the drone disappear" said Adam, now he was getting excited.

Nothing. As the drone reached 100 feet, it just hovered and there was no loud crack, no noise at all, just the sound of the blades spinning.

"I don't understand," replied Adam. "Last time, it happened when it reached 100 feet."
He decided to climb a few more feet.

At 125 feet the loud crack emitted from the sky. The drone disappeared once again.

Adam immediately looked at the small screen on the control.
"Maggie, look at this!" said Adam with excitement in his voice.

Maggie couldn't believe the scene on the screen she was watching. Adam was descending the drone slowly till he could see clearly all below.

It was the town called "Breeds" stated by the sign hanging by one nail. The sign was alongside the railroad tracks. It was hard to read but Adam made the drone hover there for a few seconds then headed towards the rest of the town. Not the community of today but about a hundred years ago, if not longer.

There it was. People pushing a mining cart coming out of a cave with two rails protruding from the opening. The people looked like ghosts.

All at once everyone, rather the ghosts, scattered. They ran back into the cave. They hid behind the carts they were pushing. There were tiny little sparks coming off the metal carts.

"What the hell?" asked Maggie. "Look, wait, those are sparks from bullets! People are dropping like flies. Somebody is killing them."

"I remember reading something about that. There was this guy that went bonkers. He went down to a mine and just started shooting, killing everyone."

"Did they ever find him?" asked Maggie.

"Nope. According to the book, they never found out who it was." replied Adam.

"Well, your drone just showed him holding what looked like a pistol and shooting people. How can that be? How can your drone show that and fly back in time?"

'I had an idea……but I am not sure." answered Adam. "What? Tell me. I don't care how ridiculous it may sound. Tell me." said Maggie. "Better yet, go back to the time you got the drone. Don't leave anything out. From the time you ordered till now," added Maggie.

"Ok," began Adam. "But first we need to get this drone back here. In today's time."

Adam took the drone back up to 125 feet. Once again there was a loud crack and the screen on the controls showed the town as it was when they arrived.

Adam placed the drone in the car and secured the case with a seat belt. "A while back I had a couple of small drones. They were nothing fancy or high tech. Their range was about one-fourth of a mile. Just something to play with. They didn't even tell you if the battery was going to die. One evening I was looking online for drones, and there were a lot of them. I didn't want the cheapest but I couldn't afford the most expensive ones. You know the ones in the thousands. I found the one I could afford. It was in the mid-range of price but seemed to have everything I wanted. I ordered it. About three weeks later it arrived. I took the box inside and began opening it. The drone itself was larger than what the picture showed, at least I thought so. It was about three feet square, with props on each corner. A package of batteries sealed in plastic. There were six "AA" batteries for the drone and four for the controller. The controller had two control sticks. One on each side, like all the others. There was a screen between them. This was so you could see where you were going and record what you could see.

    I put the batteries in and decided to go outside and check it out. I flew it around for a while getting used to the controls, sort of getting the feel of everything. Two days later we had that tremor from the earthquake. I heard it was centered in the next town, somewhere on the outskirts. I took my drone and decided to go see where it was. I stopped in town and got a little information. Apparently, the quake left a small little trench on this farmer's land. Mr. Wright was the farmer. Everyone I talked to said he was very nice and friendly. I decided to pay him a visit. After a small chat, I asked if I could fly my drone over his property and up the trench.

    They were right, he was a really nice person. He pointed towards the pasture and said it was just beyond the tree line. Told me the trench wasn't very big or very long. I thanked him and started my adventure. To me it was an adventure." Adam said to Maggie.

    "Did he go with you?" asked Maggie.

"No, he said he had chores to do, and for me to be careful," started Adam again. "He also asked if I had a cell phone"

"Why?" interrupted Maggie.

"He gave me his number; in case I got into trouble. He said "you never know".

"After walking for about half an hour, crossing the pasture and fences. I reached the tree line. I went about another ten minutes into the trees and found the small trench. Small was right. It was about a foot wide and went back and forth through the trees. It only went about; I'd say one hundred yards. I thought I had better get to flying. The sun was on the western horizon now and it would be dark soon.

Getting the drone and controls ready didn't take long. I immediately started flying the trench. Of course, I was on the bank. The sun had disappeared now and I was just about to the end of the trench when I saw something shiny up ahead.

It was coming out of the trench. Kinda looked like a very bright flashlight shining straight up towards the sky. I thought maybe someone had dropped their light down in the trench. I hovered the drone there till I could close enough to it. It was getting darker by the minute and harder to see ahead of me.

As I approached the glowing trench, I noticed it was brighter than any flashlight. Looking down in the small opening at the brightness, I reached in my pocket for my sunglasses. Putting them on didn't help. The light was way too bright. It just looked like a ball of fire, only very white. I landed the drone about ten feet away from the trench. I noticed a lightly colored kind of faded white ring around the drone. Everything seemed to be working fine, though. After about five minutes the ring disappeared.

I moved closer to the light in the trench again, but it didn't move, dim, or go out.

I started over to pick up the drone and the ground started shaking. The branches on the trees were moving side to side. The ground felt like it was shifting back and forth. I picked up the drone and stumbled around to keep my balance. It was another small quake.

With all the shaking going on, I noticed the light was a lot dimmer. Boy, did it get dark then. I pulled out my phone and used it like a flashlight. Aiming it at the location where the light had been, I saw the trench had closed back up. There was no light, no large opening, nothing but a line of fresh dirt where it had been.

I went back to the farmers house and knocked on the door. The door opened almost immediately."

Farmer Wright, was standing in the doorway and blurted out,

"Boy, am I glad to see you. I was about ready to come looking. Was going to call, but I forgot to get your number. I gave you mine but... Oh hell, you ok son?"

"Sure", I replied."

"I bet you felt that quake we had a little while ago," he said with a questioning voice.

"Yes, I did. I got something to show you. By the way, the trench closed back up. Looks like it was never there."

'What did you want to show me? asked farmer Wright."

"Wait a minute," interrupted Maggie. "Didn't he have a first name?'

"Yeah, Bob." answered Adam. "But I just like calling him farmer Wright. You know, he wasn't wrong he was always Wright"

Maggie reached out and slapped his arm. She had a small grin on her face.

"Go on," she said, shaking her head.

After viewing the video from the drone, Bob was ready to go back up there and check it out.

"Want to wait till morning?" asked Adam.

"Not really. It might be easier to spot the light in the dark," replied Bob.

Adam thought Bob was going to get some shovels as he headed for a large machine shed. Bob came around the corner on a tractor with a backhoe.

"Hop on Adam. You can leave your drone here in the house. We won't be gone long" said Bob as he brought the tractor to a halt.

Adam showed Bob where the light had been and he backed the tractor up and began digging. After about an hour and a very big hole, Bob stopped the tractor, turned off the engine and got out a flashlight.

"Well son, there doesn't seem to be anything there. At least not now. I believe you, I saw the video."

"I sure would like to know what caused the light," stated Adam as he started walking away.

"Well, we may never know," replied Bob.

Conversation lagged. Turning to Maggie, he asked.

"What should I do? I can't go to the police, they would laugh at me and just say, "Oh you doctored up the pictures."

Maggie turned to Adam with her index finger over her lips. "Just keep the drone. Use it for your own use. Sometime you may meet someone who could explain the strange light and why the drone does what it does."

"I suppose," added Adam. "But it's not normal and a little freaky."

Maggie shrugged her shoulders and started to walk away. Glancing over at the drone, her eyes got big. Her mouth opened but no sound came out. She hit Adam in the arm, and pointed.

Over where the drone was setting. A light glow was coming from around the body and the controller started humming. It never hummed while Adam was operating it.

"What now?" asked Adam, as he was hesitant about picking it up.

Both of them stood there in awe. Inquisitive but also a little scared.

Then it happened. The blades were rotating at full speed and the sticks on the controller started to move under their own power.

Was someone from a different time controlling the drone? Past or Future. We will never know. Also what about the pictures of Breeds?

DARK IMAGES

The leaves had fallen from the trees and the grass was dead and crunchy from the cold nights of December. The nights were especially cold when the sky was absent of clouds. George thought it to be the perfect time to purchase his dream TV. He told Lori that he heard of a store that was in the next town and it dealt in everything. The newspaper had said there were antiques, furniture and some things slightly used. He told her he thought the name was 'ODD THINGS, "Collections" or something like that. Lori had told him. "Then, if you want to, go for it".

It was late Saturday afternoon as George pulled up in front of the store. "Kinda reminds me of a cross between a pawn shop and an antique shop," said George, as he got out of the car.

As he entered the store he got a strange feeling from the surroundings. It was like someone or something was watching him, or it was just his imagination.

A voice came from the back of the shop somewhere. "I'll be right with you." George stood in the center of the aisle with his arms crossed, waiting.

"Hello, my name is Mark, can I help you?"

"Well," started George. After a second or two of hesitation, he continued. "I was wondering if you had a TV? Preferably a large screen. My name is George Wolf."

George was looking around and was getting a little discouraged as he looked at the items he could see.

Mark looked at George questioningly, but he could see the disappointed look on George's face. He then proceeded to speak more about the store. "I have several items here that most people buy and trade but…" He hesitated and took a deep breath, then continued. I have some "special" items in the lower room, as I call it. I believe there is a large screen TV down there. "Follow me." said Mark as he headed towards the back of the store.

As the two men approached the door that led to the lower level, they approached a spiral staircase. George started to get a tingling feeling again and asked Mark, "Why are these special items down here where nobody could see them?"

"I have felt that each item down here was meant for certain people. Like you for instance. You came looking for a large TV. Look, I have one. See what I mean?" said Mark with a slight chuckle.

"Not really. If it works, I will take it," replied George.

"You can plug it in upstairs and see if it works. I don't have electricity in this area" said Mark, as he headed towards the cardboard box back in the dusty corner.

"If you said it works, I don't need to plug it in. I'm in a hurry. Besides, if it doesn't work, I will bring it back. Ok? I do have a couple questions though", started George.

"Yes? Shoot." answered Mark sliding the cardboard box over the TV.

"Why is the screen facing the wall? And why the cardboard box?" asked George.

"Ah, both questions have the same answer. To keep the screen from getting scratched or broken", replied Mark. "Also, I have no idea of what is special about it. You sure you still want it?"

"Oh, ok. I can understand that, "stated George, as he bent down to pick up the bottom edge of the TV. "I will take it."

After they got it up the staircase, which was very difficult, they took it out to the car.

"Good thing you got a wide car," said Mark as they set it in the backseat.

"Yep. And good thing they are lighter than they used to be." added George.

"How's four hundred for the TV?" asked George.

"Oh no. How about two hundred. I don't even know if it works. Besides that, it's used," answered Mark.

"You sure?" asked George.

"Yep. Thank you and enjoy," said Mark as he extended his hand and shook George's.

"Take care, and thank you" said George as he got in his car and headed home.

The Setup

When George got home, he saw his neighbor Tim Walker outside picking up some trash that had blown into his yard.

"Hey Tim. Would you help me move a TV into the house?" asked George as he opened that back door.

"Sure George. I know they are light, but awkward," replied Tim.

Once the TV was inside and set down, Tim headed back home.

After George thanked Tim and told him goodbye, he headed back inside to remove the cardboard from the TV. He knew Lori would be late. She had told him she was going to her friends and swing by the drugstore. He knew the women got together every so often and played cards and talked about everything and everybody. George just smiled and lifted the cardboard up off the TV. Once he got the box completely removed and went to plug it into the wall, he heard a low hum.

"What? How can it be humming? I don't even have it plugged in." said George aloud.

He dropped the plug and went around to the front, looking into the screen he saw images of people moving around. They looked as if they were yelling. George looked around as if see someone standing behind him. Not a single person, just the furniture. He reached out and touched the edge of the screen.

The remote was in his other hand. There was a louder hum and George felt as if he were being drawn into the TV. It was pulling, harder and harder. The swirls spun around his body like a whirlpool. It seemed to pull harder the more he tried to resist. The remote dropped to the floor. There was silence. George was gone.

The Confusion

Lori arrived home from the drugstore. As her car approached the driveway, she noticed her husband's car pulled up close to the garage. Entering the front door, she called out for George. She placed her packages on the kitchen counter. The silence drifted through the rooms. When he didn't answer she thought maybe he had gone to the basement for tools to put the tv on a stand. Then she began to feel that something wasn't right. She couldn't really put her finger on it, though. She shook off that feeling, figuring she was just being a little paranoid. It was close to time to eat; George never missed a meal.

He would return from wherever he was pretty soon. Lori knew she would have to fix something for supper. George wouldn't cook anything on his own. Spaghetti was one of her husband's favorite meals. She pulled a pan out of the cupboard, filled it with water and put it on to boil for the noodles. Then she thought, she should at least look for George.

She searched every room before going to the garage and then in the backyard. No George. She had seen the TV and the remote on the floor. So, she knew he had already gone to that store he was talking about and had returned with his precious TV. Lori really didn't need a television. She would rather go to real places and talk to real people. After she picked up the remote from the floor, she noticed the plug to the television was laying on the floor behind it. He hadn't even bothered to plug it in before he went to wherever.

"Well, That's odd. I would think he would have plugged it in and been sitting there watching it." said Lori out loud as she plugged the cord into the wall. She then reached for the remote and turned it on and within seconds the picture appeared.

Lori wasn't interested in what was on the television right now. She was beginning to get worried about George again.

"I wonder where he could be? His car is in the driveway," remarked Lori looking towards the TV screen.

Lori searched all night for her husband. She had gone to the neighbors and asked them if they had seen him that evening. Tim told her he had helped George carry the TV inside. He also said that George had thanked him and he had gone inside. Then Tim went to his home.

Lori didn't see any sign of a disturbance. Nothing was missing in the house as far as she could tell. She didn't really think anything serious had happened, but she felt that she should call the police the next day if he didn't return home. She didn't touch anything in case the police wanted to check things over. She read a lot of crime books and sort of knew the procedure.

The Next Day

The police told her they had to wait forty-eight hours to make this a missing persons case. On the third day the police arrived and looked in all the same places Lori had. No sign of George anywhere. Lori felt they really didn't think anything was wrong, but that George had left on his own accord. She knew better.

Time went by. Lori never gave up but, no clues ever emerged regarding his disappearance. No George, no clues, not anything. If it had not been for all his clothing, his car, and other belongings, it would be as if he had never even existed at all.

The Present

Two years had passed since George's disappearance. Many tears and many lonely days and nights had passed. Lori never gave up. Hoping and praying that he would come home.

Lori just got home from shopping at the grocery store. She sat there in the car and let out a sigh. She only went once a week, the crowds of people pushing and shoving would always put her in a bad mood.

Leaning over in the car seat, she grabbed her purse and then reached up and pulled the keys out of the ignition. She knew it was going to be a struggle to get out of the car, it always was. She reached her right arm across and put her hand in the door handle. Pulling the door handle to open, she felt it drop in her hand and about broke her left shoulder pushing on it. She put the handle back on the rod and tried again. This time she used her right arm to pull on the door with a little pressure. She heard the little click and the door opened. Reaching over in the passenger's seat, she grabbed her bag of essentials.

Once outside of the car she gave the door a push. There was a loud squeak along with a creak as the car door shut. The old Chevy Belair had seen a lot of miles and the baby blue paint was fading badly. Lori called it her portable trash can and told everyone she had to clean it up, but seldom did.

She headed up the three steps to her apartment door. Fighting to get the key in the lock, she thought she better set the groceries down. Knowing this door and lock needed some extra care also when trying to open it. Once she had accomplished that, she took the bag in and set it on the table. This was the part she didn't care for. Her husband George used to come out and help her put things away, she still had those memories.

She always thought he did that, looking for treats she may have bought him. Occasionally, he was right and find a candy bar of his favorite kind in the bottom of the sack. As she stood there she began thinking back in time. She recalled what the police had told her. There was no trace of foul play or anything suspicious. The local police even called in the FBI. They too couldn't find a trace. They told her he must have just left. There just wasn't any other explanation that they could come up with.

Lori knew better. They never fought in their forty years of marriage. They went everywhere together since they were both retired, except the grocery store.

George never bought very much for himself, he wasn't into things like guns, knives and sporting goods. He did want one thing and that was a big screen TV. He had saved a little back each month, in order to buy one. That was all now in the past. She now came to reality.

After he disappeared, she decided to move to an apartment. Lori didn't want the responsibilities of mowing the grass and fixing the fence, or any of the repairs a house and yard needed, so she moved to a one-bedroom apartment. She hired a moving company to move what she wanted to keep. The rest she sold or gave away to friends. She and George didn't have any children, so she didn't have to save anything for them. She decided that she had to take the TV tough. After all, George may want to watch it when he returned.

Life goes on

Lori thought the tv had been sitting next to the wall long enough. She decided to turn it around and see if it even worked. In the past two years she hadn't touched it, it was George's. Lori had been using a small portable to watch a few shows. She wasn't much of a tv watcher, she would rather read a good book or visit with her friends.

She slowly turned the big screen around and removed the cardboard which was falling apart from the years of just sitting there. She remembered feeling a slight tingle when she leaned on the TV to pick up the remote. She had quickly pulled her hand away from the screen. Lori had turned the TV pointing towards her couch. She walked back to her seat, then picked up the remote and was ready to turn it on. She hadn't plugged it in yet but what she saw next, sent a chill down her back.

The screen was still black, but there were images moving around. They were like ghosts caught up in the screen. They were moving. They seemed to be moving back and forth with arms and hands stretched out in front of them, like they were trying to feel or was searching for something.

As Lori kept watching, she thought she saw an image that looked like George. As she walked towards the screen, she realized it was George.

"How in the world did he get in there?" she said aloud.

"George!" she yelled. But there was no reply, the images just kept moving back and forth on the TV screen.

The television was humming and getting louder the closer she got. She thought, "What am I going to do? Nobody will believe me".

She saw George's image come by again. She reached out. She touched the screen. There was the sound of an electric static, like the sound of clothes just pulled out of the dryer. The sound was loud. Then silence. Now the room was empty. Lori was no longer in front of the TV. She was in it.

The Disappearance

A couple days passed and the neighbors became concerned. They called the police and asked if they would do a well-being check.

They arrived at the apartment within ten minutes. They knocked on the door several times. Getting no answer, they put their ears up to the door to listen inside. Nothing.

The apartment manager just happened to be driving by and noticed the commotion as several of the tenets were standing around. Wondering what was going on since, she saw the police car parked out in front of the building. Pulling over to the curb and flagging a policeman down, she asked one of the officers what was going on.

"Just checking on one of your tenants. Someone was concerned that they hadn't seen any movement in a couple days. They called and asked us to check it out," said the officer as he looked down and saw the manager holding a bunch of keys on her belt.

"Want me to open it?" she asked as she reached for her keys.

"Would you, please? Might save us from breaking it down" said the policeman motioning towards the door.

Once inside they began calling out her name. There was no answer. They searched every room; all they found was the TV was off and the remote on the floor in front of it. They checked all the rooms in the apartment. No Lori.

The Case

"Hey, wasn't this the lady that lost her husband a few years back? They never found him or a trace of him. Kinda strange don't you think," said Carl, looking at the other officer.

Both officers had been on the force for about fifteen years. Carl was forty-three and his partner was forty-six. Both had been in the case of "missing George".

"Well, I suppose we better call in the Feds again since this is the wife of missing George", said Ralph

"There is something about this that feels weird," added Ralph.

"They are going to love us. They haven't solved the first one yet", replied Carl, with a huge sigh. "I agree with you though. It does make me get weird feelings about the whole situation"

"What am I supposed to do now?" asked Kim, the manager. She had been the manager with her husband Bob for about sixteen years. They remembered the case about Lori's husband and just figured he left Lori and was probably in some other state or country.

Amos Black

Amos Black had been a private investigator for thirty-five years and had some strange cases, but he was beginning to think this was the strangest. No clues, no evidence of foul play, no witnesses, nothing to go on. At first, he thought the wife could be the guilty one. Then about two years later the wife shows up missing.

Amos enjoyed cases like this, ones that made him think. This one may be just that type. Every time he would come up with an idea, he would run into a dead end. He would rub his bald head and continue on. He would often do this when he thought about retiring. Being 59, he knew he was getting close. His body was starting to show a few years on it. He had a wife once. Evelyn was a year younger but she passed three years ago from cancer. Amos really missed her and tried to keep busy to occupy his mind.

Back at his office, Amos sat in his chair which would lean to one side. The wheels would snag every so often and about throw him out on the floor. He leaned back cautiously and put his feet up on his wooden desk. With the file in hand and the pictures of the house and apartment building, where the two had disappeared, two years apart. He began to look through all the information he had gathered.

Amos wanted his office away from others. Said he could think better and besides his father used to be a detective and had this office. It saved on paying rent or making payments. It was downtown near an old industrial park. Amos really liked the solitude he got in the office.

Time to think

He noticed that Lori was a neat nick. Everything was picked up and neatly put away in its place. From the pictures, it was the same condition as the house her and her husband lived in together, very orderly.

Then why the remote on the floor and not on the stand beside the chair? Also in both pictures, the clock on the wall showed six- o-five. The same clock was on the wall in their house and it too showed six- o-five.

"Hey, I don't know what it means, yet, but it's a start, " said Amos rubbing his chin and leaning forward in the chair.

"Then again, the clock could have some meaning to her and never run since that time. Maybe it's broken, or dead batteries, or... shit, now I'm grasping at straws."

He looked back at the pictures once more. This time he looked at the TV. "Seems kind of strange that the TV in the apartment and in their house was unplugged. I know the neighbors said she liked the quiet and would hardly ever watch TV. But why was it unplugged? It was also unplugged when her husband disappeared. There I go again grasping at straws."
He put the file and pictures on the desk and walked over to his window. The view wasn't the greatest. It looked across the alley at the other building's brick wall. Not even a window looking into an office that he could peer into. He wasn't a pervert, but it would beat a solid brick wall.

A small bat slammed into the window, causing a tiny chip in the glass. Of course, Amos jumped back about half a step. He had been in a state of thought about the case and the sudden jolt knocked him back to reality.

Amos slowly reached up to his shirt pocket to get a cigarette and pulling out the pack he turned it over to shake out one of his stress relief sticks. This is what he called them. He put the cigarette up to his lips and put the pack back then reached for his lighter. It slipped between his fingers and fell to the floor.

A Clue

As he bent over, he noticed a dark window on his apartment cooler he kept cold drinks in.

"Oh shit!" he said looking at the dark glass on the cooler. "What the hell? I saw my reflection in the glass and something else in the reflection. An image I know wasn't in my office."

Amos went back to his desk and pulled out the pictures of the big screen TV. After looking over them with a magnifying glass. He set down the glass and dropped the picture.

"I have to go back to that apartment tomorrow", Amos said as he lit his cigarette he had been holding in his lips for about fifteen minutes.

He took a long drag and slowly exhaled. Being in a state of bewilderment, Amos didn't want to believe this was something unexplainable, like a science fiction, alien thing.

Once back in his chair he pulled out his phone. There on the dark screen was images. They looked like people but he wasn't sure. He only knew that there was nothing in his office moving and these images were. He slightly moved the phone and the time appeared and the images disappeared.

Re-visit

The next day, Amos returned to Lori's apartment. He had called the police and received permission to look around again.

Once inside he went to the TV and decided to check it out closer. He reached down and plugged it in. There was a faint humming sound. Amos had picked up the remote and had turned it on.

"Doesn't look like there is anything wrong with it," Amos said aloud.

He gripped the remote and pointed at the TV to turn it off. Once the picture disappeared the humming returned. Amos unplugged the cord from the wall and the humming continued. He backed up about three feet from the screen. The humming subsided somewhat.

He sat down on the couch and looked at the screen. The dark images were moving all around.

"Oh, hell no," he said aloud. "This can't be. Come on, these things only happen in movies or in books. Not for real."

Amos reached for his pocket and pulled his phone out. He was in awe. The images were exactly like the ones on the big TV screen. They moved at the same time and in the same directions. He put his phone back in his pocket and decided to go to the police station and show them what he discovered.

The Prank

Amos entered the police station. He asked to see Captain Simms.

"Be just a minute. Oh wait, you can go in now," said the officer behind the desk, as an elderly man just came out of the captain's office.

Amos and Ned Sims had been friends since grade school. Ned ran his fingers through his very thin gray hair trying to cover the baldness.

"Amos, what brings you here?" Ned asked as he shook his head in a negative manner and smiled.

"What's so funny?" asked Amos as he took a chair.

"Old man Jacobs, the guy that just left, said he was hearing very faint voices. They were in his apartment. Nobody lived next door," said Ned as he pulled his chair up to the desk.

"You are going to think I'm crazy, but I went back over to the apartment and discovered something I can't explain," said Amos as he reached for his phone. He laid it on the desk with the screen down.

"Well, what you got?" asked the captain, getting a little impatient.

Amos reached down and turned the phone over and the face lit up with the time and temperature.

"Yes? I'm waiting. What are you going to show me that you discovered", said Ned as he looked at the phone. "I got a clock on the wall."

"Wait till the face fades away," added Amos. The numbers disappeared and images were moving about on the dark screen.

"What kind of stupid prank are you trying to pull?" asked Ned.

"None. Give me your phone," said Amos as he put his hand out.

Amos put Ned's phone on the desk next to his. The images appeared in Ned's phone after the screen went black.

"What the hell?" asked Ned, standing there in awe.

Amos called one of the other officers to bring their phone in. The same thing happened to his. The images were moving exactly as the other two. They were in unison.

The Explanation

"Now this may sound stupid or even crazy. I was over at the apartment and I saw those images in that big TV Mrs. Wolf had.

The same images appeared on my phone. I looked closely at them and from the photographs I believe I found Lori and her husband in the TV. They were reaching out, like they were asking for help."

Ned stood there for a minute, not saying a word.

"Like I said, this has to be some kind of prank, joke. I don't care.

Just take your dark images and get out of here before I lock you up."

Amos picked up his phone and without arguing he left. Once he was outside, he heard the roar of laughter as Ned was telling the others in the station.

Amos thought it over as he was heading back to the office,

"Ah hell, I'm going back to the apartment. I don't care what Ned said. There is something wrong there. I am going to try and figure it out. Maybe I can get those trapped out of what looks like a living hell," said Amos as he headed for the apartment and the big TV.

Amos parked in the driveway and went to the apartment door. There was tape across the doorway but the door wasn't locked. He thought that was a little odd, but maybe the tape discouraged any thieves.

Amos headed inside. There it was sitting in the middle of the living room. The big screen TV was unplugged but still humming. It sent a small chill down his back but he figured it was some chipboard holding power. He didn't know anything about electronics.

He picked up the remote and pointed it towards the big screen. Amos didn't press the button; he wanted to see the images on the dark screen once again.

He wasn't thinking. Amos leaned on the screen trying to get a closer look at the people. The remote dropped to the floor. Amos was now among the missing. He had become one of the "Dark Images"

The Conclusion

Take a look at your TV. Is it off? Look closer. Do you see Lori, George, or Amos? If you do, you may want to turn it on without touching the TV itself.

Oh, by the way dark images may appear anywhere. Wonder who they are? Know anyone that is missing?

Couple questions. Do you own a cell phone?
Look at the black screen, see anyone you know?

CYBER-HUMAN

They searched my room last night. When I returned from trying to find something to eat, my room had been turned upside down. I must stay in the dark at night and out of sight in the daylight. Even the smallest of children are out there looking for me. So far, I've managed to stay one step ahead of them. I know sooner or later they will find me and it will be all over. If there are any more like me out there; please run! Run for your life!

It really began when I was very young. All through my life it has seemed like I was all alone. People have changed for some reason. Unexplained, but still changed. They work harder and longer. They always seemed to be like zombies. They didn't have friendly conversation. I never knew the real reason I felt this way until a few days ago when I discovered what they really are.

I don't think they are humans. They seem to be mere replicas. They could be considered a robot built to the most advanced state. They look like humans but yet each one is actually different on the inside in some weird way. I had to find out how. This I knew would be a risky task, but luck was with me.

This happened about a week ago. I was driving down Interstate 74 with not a care in the world. I was happy and singing to the radio. It had been raining for the past two weeks, off and on, and this was the first day of real sunshine. The sky was a deep blue and the sun was beating down on the pavement causing gizmos to form.

When I rounded a curve in the highway, I saw the red lights flashing. A blue station wagon was turned over on its crumpled top. I saw that the occupants were still trapped in the car. I slowed down, as the state trooper had waved his hand and pointed to the other lane.

As I drove past the station wagon, I glanced over at the upturned car. An arm was sticking out of the driver's window. I could see the blood covered muscles from the open cut. But what really caught my eye were the sparks that jumped from a point in the gash in the driver's head. I told myself I must have seen something else. It couldn't really have been sparks.

I pulled over, stopped my car, and started walking. When I got back to the wreck, I looked at the arm and head once again. At first, I had thought I was imagining things but now that I saw it again, I realized it was true. Sparks were flowing up and down the head! There was also a piece of shiny metal glistening in the sunlight from the victim's neck. I had seen this very same thing once before but under different circumstances.

Immediately I put two and two together and looked at the trooper. He must have realized what I was looking at. He tossed a blanket over the body and raised up to look at me. I realized that I had already seen too much. I began to walk away but when I got far enough back from them, I ran for my car.

The trooper yelled for me to stop. Usually, I would have done what a state trooper told me to do. But not this time. I had to get out of there. I hopped in my car and threw gravel behind me as I floored the accelerator. I had gotten several miles down the road before I saw the flashing red lights appear in my rearview mirror. I was like an escaped convict. I didn't know where to go. I had no other person to turn to. My worst fear had come true! I was alone in this world.

I mean really alone and running. If there were others out there like me, I didn't know where. I did realize however, that the ones that were chasing me had to be like the one in the car and they were all over the place. Could it be robots and not humans that were running the country? The world?

I pulled off the road and quickly abandoned the car. I was in the middle of the woods. It should be easy to lose the trooper. I walked through the woods until I came to a small house. I hid behind the buildings for two hours until I saw some movement. A small child came out of the house carrying a pail. Apparently, he was going to do some chores. I whispered to him to come to me. He dropped the pail and ran to the house yelling: "That guy is out here! He is behind the shed!"

On the run

Almost immediately two adults, which I assumed to be the child's parents, came running out. The man was carrying a large club, which I presumed was meant for me. I returned to the cover of the woods. They didn't follow. I have only to guess they went for help. That evening, I ate some wild grapes and some berries. It wasn't much, but at least I wouldn't starve. I found a house where nobody was home. Yes, I became a criminal. I broke in took a quick shower grabbed a bite of food and some clothes that were a little big on me but they were clean. Just as I left through the back door, the occupants of the house pulled into the driveway. I ran as fast as I could towards the woods again.

The next day I was drinking from the stream that ran through the woods. I raised up just in time to see a cloud of some milky looking substance come floating down the stream. I knew I had to leave. With no water, I wouldn't survive long. Apparently, I thought, they had gotten up stream and poisoned the water. I waited until the cover of night and then made my escape.

I walked to the edge of the wooded area and looked the situation over. There they were, standing about ten feet apart waiting for me to appear. Thankfully they were looking just a little past from where I had emerged. I thought it would be almost impossible to escape them, until I spotted a small ravine. The trees were casting a shadow over it. There were two of them, one on each side. I figured if I moved slowly and quietly, I could get out undetected. It would be risky, but it was the only way out I could see.

As I slid along the bank hoping not to attract their attention, I peered up over the edge. I could have sworn I was past them by now, but the sight of brown shoes made me realize that I was right beside them again. Edging my way along in the dark, groping at the exposed roots, I finally managed to get far enough along the ravine that I could climb out and run for cover.

Once again, I broke into a vacant house and obtained some clothes and a little food. Now I knew how an escaped convict felt. The ever-present danger of doing the wrong thing and letting them find me. I hear the sirens off in the distance. I must escape! I just hope that if there is another real human out there somewhere, they find me or I find them before the cyborgs (that's what I decided to call them) did.

Heading for the City

After I left their little search party behind, I headed for the city, which was about twenty miles down the road. Staying off to the side of the road and under cover I managed to reach the edge of the city before the sun came up.

I was exhausted by the time I found an old culvert that went under the main highway leading into the city. Here I hoped to rest up until the safety of darkness came once again. My feet were aching from all the running and dodging. I slept for what I considered to be about eight hours. My watch had fallen off sometime during my escape and I didn't know the exact time. The sun was in the western sky and I had to estimate the distance to the horizon to know how much time there was before sunset.

My stomach was growling and I knew that I had to find food. Reaching in my billfold, I found that I had only a twenty-dollar bill left. I wondered if I should risk it. Take a chance and try to get something to eat at a nearby cafe. I figured I could saunter in like nothing had ever happened and see how things went. After reaching the cafe. I walked in and sat at the table. A few people were eating, but they didn't seem to pay any attention to me. So far so good. The waitress walked over and asked me for my order.

I ordered a hamburger and hoped they could have it cooked and served before I got discovered. I was totally surprised when they brought my meal within twenty minutes and told me to enjoy it. That I did. Even though it was just a hamburger, it was good until I was on my last bite.

The Escape

The waitress walked over and asked me if I would like another cup of coffee. When I said yes, I expected her to pour it. I looked up from my plate and saw why she hadn't. In the doorway stood the cops. Almost immediately, everyone in the cafe stopped eating and looked from the cops to me. They all knew! I looked around for an escape route. There was a door which was next to the door that went to the kitchen. It read fire exit.

I took off from my table and dodged the people and tables and chairs as I bolted through the exit door. To my surprise I ran into another cop! I should have expected him. How did they know I was there? I kept asking them. They wouldn't answer. Just directed me to their squad car. Inside the car was one patrolman sitting at the wheel. Placing me in the back seat, they shut the door. They didn't handcuff me.

(I don't have much time, so I must tell my story).

The patrolman started the car and drove away with me in the back. Once we were moving, I knew I had to try to escape. I put both hands together and clenched them tight. I swung as hard as I could and hit the patrolman in the back of the head. Sparks flew and his head fell forward on the steering wheel.

I had short circuited him. That had to be their vulnerable spot. I didn't try to see what he looked like. The car was careening down the street. We hit a building. My head hit something on impact and I was unconscious for a few seconds. When I came to, the car was smoking and dust was still settling.

I managed to crawl out of the window and clear the wreck and the building. Once I was on the street, I looked around to see if anyone was nearby. The only person was a pregnant lady. She ignored the whole incident as if it hadn't happened.

I didn't wait around to see anything else. I ran down the street. I knew they would be there in a matter of minutes. If they caught me again, they wouldn't make the same mistake of not cuffing me. I knew they had to have found out that I had escaped. The street lights were starting to come on. It would soon be dark, then I hoped I could move about a little safer. As I stood in an alley, hiding behind some crates, I began thinking about that pregnant woman. I didn't know why, but her condition really confused me. If she was one of them, how was she pregnant?

I waited until dark. Then I went out the back way of the alley. I had no idea where I was going. I just wanted to get away and be left alone. I stayed out of sight as much as possible until I was sure most of the people had gone to bed, or whatever they did. I really didn't know what they wanted from me or what they would do with me. I wasn't going to stick around and find out either.

I could hear the sirens again. It seemed that the sound was headed in my direction. I didn't know if they would stop or not this time. I'm going to make this story as short as I can. I feel my luck and time is about to run out.

The alley came out near the side of a hospital. I stood there for a few minutes, assessing the situation. I was about ready to take a step when a car came down the street. I ducked into the shadows of a large garbage container and stayed until I was sure of where the car was going. Apparently, they weren't interested in me, because the car pulled into the Emergency entrance to the hospital. I stayed hidden and watched a woman emerge from the passenger's side. Another pregnant woman. "How?"

The pregnant lady

As I stood there the answer hit me. Robots were always made. How could this woman be carrying a child? I didn't know if it was an act to fool me or not. I knew that I had to find out what was going on. I entered the hospital, avoiding every person I could. It wasn't too difficult as it was at night. I hid in stairways, closets, and laundry rooms. Working my way through the hospital until I came to the maternity ward.

A woman was having a child. I could tell by the groans from labor pains coming from the delivery room. I wasn't supposed to be there, but I eased the door open. I saw that it wasn't the woman who came in earlier but a different one. As I stood there, I saw the doctor lift the baby and placed it in a large plastic pan, which was lined with white linen. I followed the nurse carrying the pan. She didn't take the baby to a nursery like I always thought they did. Instead, she took it to an operating room where doctors and nurses were waiting for it.

The operating room was equipped with one of those viewing decks, where young doctors watch an operation, to learn, and discover new techniques. Without revealing myself, I managed to sneak to this observation deck and watch what they were going to do to this infant. I found a nurse's jacket and put it on over my clothes, so I wouldn't stand out too much.

After preparing the child, they opened its skull and planted what looked like a small TV circuit board at the base of its head.

After the scalp was closed back up, the nurse went over to a rather large computer looking machine and started running it. My God! They were programming the child's brain! Immediately, I reached for the back of my head to feel if I had a scar or anything. Nothing. This must be the reason they were chasing me. Why was I different?

I left the hospital totally confused. I ran most of the way through the city. Stopping only long enough to catch my breath and look for the police. As I was running past, I looked for one car that still had the keys in it. I had never stolen a car before. I had to get out of this place and find out why I wasn't like them. I finally found a car with the keys still in the ignition.

Driving all night and thinking about the things that had been happening to me cleared my head. I remembered the town where I was born. I knew I had to start there. My own birth. It took me two days to get there. I drove at night and slept during the day. I stole gas from farmers. I was very lucky and never got caught.

Finally, reaching the town I was born in, I went to the hospital. I waited until I had a chance and darted through the corridors until I found a room that had records written on the door. It was locked, of course. Without being noticed, I tried every way possible to get in. Finally, I decided to go outside and come through the window. I would break it if I had to, but I had to see my records. I didn't know what I was looking for, but I had to look.

I stayed in the shadows once again and slipped over to the window. I found the window was open about three inches. I had thought I would have to break the glass, since the door was locked and everything was supposed to be secured on the inside. I reached up and pushed the window the rest of the way open and climbed inside. I heard footsteps outside the room. I just need a few more minutes.

I opened the cabinet with a letter opener I found lying on a desk. I fumbled through the folders and drawers until I found my records. My God! I was supposed to get one of those microchips too! It shows here that my mother stole me when I was an infant.

Maybe that is why they take the child as soon as it is born now. They don't want to take any more chances. Reading on, I found why they were chasing me: Victim should be apprehended at once! This was stamped across the last page of my birth record followed by the death notice of my mother.

How had I managed to stay out of reach for thirty-two years?

The capture

"I hear voices outside my door. They are calling me out. They have found me. I wanted more time. It has run out. If there are any more of you out there like me, run for your life. They are ramming the door now. The hinges just gave way. There are only three of them...maybe, just maybe. I was no match for them. One pulled my arm out straight from my side. The other held my other arm. The third was a woman in a nurse's outfit. She had a needle, a very big needle. It was pushed into the side of my neck. I felt the sting, then everything went dark.

When I woke, I saw a, let's call them cyber-humans. Half human, half cyborg. Sitting in a chair next to my bed. He had that blank stare, so I knew he was one of them. I reached up to my head and felt the bandage. They had gotten me. I looked up in time to see what I presumed to be a tech carrying a laptop. I knew they were going to program the chip they had put in my head.

The Warning

Ever sit at a restaurant and have someone sitting across the room stare at you? I mean a blank stare. No smile, no nod of the head or look away, then immediately look back and stare at you? Run! Run as fast as you can. I put this whole story and message in my phone, hoping someone could recover it later. Thank you. I see you got my phone. Cell phones are no longer needed. They communicate between each other, like a giant electronic net around the world. They tossed mine on the table and ignored it.
I was able to grab it and put out this final warning before they reprogram me. Hide, run, and trust no one.

Side Effect

The day unfolded like any other in the heart of fall, crisp and invigorating in the early hours before the sun warmed the air to a pleasant temperature. Doug had decided to escape to the timber once again, seeking the quiet solace the woods reliably provided. Over the summer, these trips had become a personal ritual, a way to unplug from the demands of life and immerse himself in the serenity of nature. Each visit left him refreshed, though the persistent annoyance of mosquitoes occasionally tested his patience.

The path Doug followed had grown familiar, its dirt surface worn smooth by his frequent footsteps. Although the area was part of a state park, it was rarely visited, and many of the trails had begun to succumb to the encroaching undergrowth. Vines and bushes crept closer to the edges, and grasses swayed tall in the breeze, evidence of the trail's quiet abandonment. This lack of traffic was a blessing in disguise, ensuring a tranquil escape where Doug could feel utterly alone with his thoughts.

As he walked, the forest around him seemed to wrap him in a cocoon of calm. The towering trees muted the outside world, creating an auditory sanctuary where the only sounds were those of nature. He paused to take in the gentle rhythm of the woods: the soft rustle of leaves as squirrels darted through the underbrush, the steady chorus of crickets hidden among the shadows, and the melodic swaying of branches in the breeze. In the distance, the stream added its voice to the woodland symphony, its water bubbling over smooth stones as it carved a meandering path through a tangle of oak, maple, and elm trees.

Doug found himself drawn to the water, where the interplay of light and sound felt almost meditative. The scene was simple yet deeply profound, a reminder of the timeless beauty found in moments of stillness. The world beyond the timber seemed far away, and for now, that was exactly what he wanted.

As Doug stood by the stream, his attention was drawn to a faint movement out of the corner of his eye. He could have sworn he saw the branches of a weeping willow shift unnaturally, as though something had deliberately pushed them aside—not the wind. A subtle tension settled over him as he turned his head slowly, careful not to make any abrupt motions that might disturb whatever was there. His gaze lingered on the spot where he thought he had seen the disturbance, but the scene appeared undisturbed. The willow's branches swayed gently, animated only by the breeze.

After a moment, Doug chuckled to himself, shaking off the unease. Probably just a squirrel, he thought, envisioning the tiny creature darting out of sight, playing an unintentional game of hide-and-seek. With a light smile tugging at his lips, he turned his attention back to the water.

The stream, with its steady flow, offered a soothing rhythm. A small pool had formed at a bend, where the current slowed, creating a perfect haven for minnows. He watched as the tiny fish darted lazily through the clear water, their silvery scales catching the light in fleeting glimmers. The momentary distraction of nature's simplicity helped to ground him, easing his mind as he stood there, letting the peace of the scene wash over him.

There it was again. This time, he caught the faintest flicker in his peripheral vision, just enough to confirm its presence but not enough to discern its nature. The movement was brief and elusive, vanishing almost as quickly as it appeared. Doug froze for a moment, his senses on high alert, scanning the area in the hope of seeing more. He turned his head slightly, careful not to make any sudden movements, but the woods around him seemed to hold their breath, offering no further hints.

Determined to get a better look, he cautiously stepped downstream, keeping close to the edge of the water. The stream's gentle babbling provided a subtle backdrop as he advanced, his eyes darting back and forth in search of any sign of motion. He paused every few steps, straining to detect even the slightest disturbance among the trees or the underbrush. Still, the forest remained silent and still, as if whatever had been there had melted into the shadows.

Frustration crept in as he realized his efforts were in vain. Despite his focus and careful movements, nothing stirred. Whatever it was, if it had even been anything at all, was gone now, leaving Doug with nothing but questions and the faint feeling that he had imagined it all.

Doug lingered there for what felt like an eternity, though it was only about fifteen minutes. His eyes strained to focus on the far edges of his peripheral vision, fixating on the leftmost corner as if expecting some elusive shape to reappear. The tension was almost comical, and he mused to himself that if he kept this up, his eyes might stay locked in that position permanently. Despite his efforts, nothing stirred in the shadows or danced across the edges of his sight. The stillness of the scene was both calming and frustrating.

Eventually, with a soft sigh, he crouched down and picked up half of a hickory shell from the ground, its ridges rough and cool against his fingertips. He studied it for a moment before tossing it into the water, watching as ripples expanded outward, disturbing the glassy surface of the stream. The motion felt like a quiet punctuation to his watchful waiting. Deciding it was time to move on, Doug turned and began to retrace his steps along the winding path he had followed to reach this spot, the rhythmic crunch of leaves beneath his feet a welcome reminder of the steady, predictable passage of time.

Doug was in his early forties, a stage of life where the years subtly began to leave their mark. His dark brown hair, though still present in respectable volume, was beginning to thin noticeably, particularly at the crown where a bald spot had begun to claim its territory. Each year, it seemed to expand just a little more, a quiet testament to the passage of time. His eyesight remained serviceable enough to avoid the need for glasses, though he occasionally found himself squinting, particularly in dim light or when trying to focus on small details.

Standing just short of six feet tall—five feet eleven, to be exact—Doug had the unremarkable build of an average middle-aged man. His frame carried a bit more weight than it once did, with a modest roll settling over the waistband of his pants. While it wasn't a drastic change, it was enough to serve as a reminder of slower metabolism and the busy years that left little room for the physical activity of his youth.

As he ascended the slope leading back from the stream, his breathing grew noticeably heavier, each step requiring a bit more effort than he liked to admit. The incline, though gentle, seemed to amplify his awareness of his physical state, a minor but persistent signal that age was catching up. Still, he pressed on, his pace steady, the sound of his footsteps mingling with the faint rustling of leaves and the distant murmur of the stream behind him.

The movement appeared once more, this time so close it seemed to be just a couple of feet behind him. Startled, Doug spun around, his eyes scanning the woods with heightened urgency. Once more, there was nothing—only the silent, unyielding trees and the faint rustling of leaves in the breeze.

Doug was not the kind of man to be easily unnerved. Practical and level-headed, he prided himself on his ability to stay composed in unsettling situations. But whatever was stalking him now, whatever seemed to toy with him, was beginning to chip away at his calm demeanor. He could feel it—an unwelcome presence, just out of reach, moving deliberately beyond his sight.

As he reached the path, Doug paused, glancing around and peering back through the trees in search of a clue. The clearing he had just passed through looked untouched, the grass and leaves undisturbed, as though he had imagined the entire encounter. But the feeling in his gut told him otherwise. He turned to continue along the trail when something caught his eye—a flicker of movement ahead, just down the path. He froze, his gaze locking on the spot. And then it vanished.

A split second later, it reappeared off to his right, darting between the trees before disappearing again. Then to his left. Then behind him. Doug's pulse quickened as the realization struck him: whatever this was, it was circling him. The trees seemed to aid its movements, offering perfect cover as it darted from one hiding place to the next. He turned his head slightly, trying to follow the motion, but the moment he shifted his gaze, it had already moved again. The thing—or perhaps things—was outmaneuvering him, as though testing his defenses, looking for an opening.

A chill ran down his spine as the hair on the back of his neck stood on end. For the first time, Doug felt genuinely frightened—not of something tangible, but of an unseen predator that didn't want to be seen. The sense of vulnerability was suffocating, and his confusion about what to do only made the feeling worse.

Desperate for some sense of control, Doug reached down and grabbed a dead branch from the ground beneath an elm tree. The wood was rough and solid in his hands, a small but reassuring weapon. He swung it in a wide arc, striking the side of the tree with a forceful crack that echoed through the woods, breaking off the tip of the branch. The sharp sound shattered the quiet, and for a moment, he hoped it might scare off whatever was stalking him.

But the oppressive sense of being watched didn't lift. The presence remained, flitting through the shadows just beyond his line of sight, too fast and too elusive for him to catch. Doug's fear deepened. He could handle being afraid of something visible—something he could confront or fight. But this... this was different. This was calculated, intentional, and unrelenting.

Doug stood frozen, gripping the branch tightly as his mind raced. He didn't know what it was or what it wanted, but one thing was certain: it was not going to let him leave without a fight.

"Maybe if I ran for it, I could outpace it. Or maybe, if it saw me leaving, it would lose interest and let me go," Doug thought, his mind racing as fast as his pulse. He started up the path cautiously, his pace slow and deliberate at first. Then he quickened his steps, testing his theory. Before long, he broke into a full sprint, his legs pumping with a desperation that overpowered his usual sense of reason. Too many maybes, he thought bitterly. And this will be a dead run if I don't slow down.

Doug's heart pounded violently in his chest, a deep drumbeat that drowned out the sounds of the forest. Sweat streamed down his face, chilling his skin despite the warmth of the day. He couldn't help but think how all those afternoons spent jogging around the local football field were finally paying off. But he knew—he felt—that it wasn't enough. It was still after him. He could sense it, like an invisible force closing in, its presence tightening the air around him. The terror of tripping and falling filled his mind, the certainty that if he went down, the creature—or creatures—would be on him in an instant.

As he crested the first hill, Doug's thoughts turned to the big oak tree that had fallen across the path further ahead. He considered diving behind it, using it as a barrier to catch his breath and maybe, just maybe, see what was chasing him. But second thoughts followed quickly. If it hasn't caught me yet, why stop? The risk seemed too great. He pressed forward, the memory of the tree now serving only as a marker for how far he had come—or how far he might fall.

The massive oak finally came into view, its sprawling trunk a daunting obstacle across the trail. Doug scrambled to climb over it, his hands gripping the rough bark for balance. Just as he was halfway across, he felt it—a sudden, fleeting touch brushing the back of his neck. Instinctively, he swiped at it, his hand batting at empty air. The motion threw off his balance, and he tumbled forward, crashing to the ground with a force that drove the air from his lungs.

Dazed and breathless, Doug lay sprawled on his back, staring up at the canopy of trees above. The limbs swayed gently against the pale sky, a stark contrast to the chaos unfolding around him. That's when he saw them—what had been chasing him.

Small creatures, grotesque and savage, swarmed over him with terrifying speed. They clawed at his clothes, their sharp teeth slicing through the fabric as if it were paper. Wherever they bit, they tore away flesh with razor precision, sending waves of searing pain coursing through his body. Doug screamed as a fiery stab shot up his leg, the agony so intense it nearly paralyzed him. He tried to push them off, to fight back, but there were too many. Dozens of them, perhaps more, clawing, biting, tearing.

The creatures resembled monstrous rats, walking upright on two legs with hunched, sinewy bodies. Their eyes gleamed with malevolent hunger, and their mouths were full of sharp, glistening teeth, each bite accompanied by a sickening rip of flesh. Doug turned his head just in time to see one lunging for his neck, its jaw gaping wide, yellowish saliva dripping from its fangs. The bite came with excruciating force, a fiery pain that seemed to explode through his entire body.

Blood sprayed in vivid arcs, staining the ground and the creatures that feasted on him. Doug tried to yell, his voice raw and desperate, but the woods swallowed his cries. No one was nearby to hear him—he was completely alone. The world around him began to blur as the pain overwhelmed him, the trees spinning wildly above before fading into darkness.

In his final moments of consciousness, Doug's mind raced with a single, haunting realization: he had no chance. The creatures had him pinned, their savage attack unstoppable. The forest fell silent once more as

Doug slipped into the void, his body broken and bloodied beneath the ancient trees.

About ten minutes later, Doug slowly regained consciousness, his head spinning. He instinctively reached for his neck, fingers grazing the skin as he searched for any sign of injury. To his disbelief, there were no bite marks, no scratches—nothing. His hands trembled as he looked at them, expecting to see blood or torn flesh, but there was nothing. His clothes were intact, no sign of the attack he had felt so vividly just moments ago.

Doug pushed himself into a sitting position, scanning the area with growing confusion. The creatures—whatever they were—had vanished. There was no trace of them, no evidence that they had ever been there. The forest around him seemed unchanged, the stillness almost mocking his terror. A squirrel chattered away from a nearby branch, and a few birds flitted from tree to tree, their wings flapping softly in the quiet. Everything seemed perfectly ordinary.

He stood up shakily, brushing off his jeans. Once again, he marveled at how undisturbed they were. Not a tear, not a scratch. He couldn't make sense of it.

"What the hell is going on?" Doug muttered, his voice strained with confusion as he looked around, hoping for some clue to explain the bizarre events. His only response was the squirrel, which paused to stare at him for a moment before resuming its chatter. The birds had flown off to another tree, their quiet movements almost taunting him with their normalcy.

Doug's gaze drifted toward the tree he had been lying beside. A small, incredulous grin tugged at the corner of his lips as he considered the possibility that it had all been a dream. Maybe I hit my head when I fell, he thought, trying to rationalize the unexplainable. Maybe I just had a really bad dream while I was knocked out.

He reached up and felt his scalp, expecting to find a bump or bruise where he had hit the ground. But there was nothing—no knot, no pain. Just smooth skin.

"I know all of that couldn't have been a dream," Doug mumbled to himself, rubbing his forehead as if the action might somehow bring clarity. The more he thought about it, the less convinced he became.

With a frustrated shake of his head, Doug decided it was best to leave the woods and head home. He wasn't going to get answers here. Without another word, he started walking back, his pace quickening into a jog. Then, instinctively, he broke into a run, his legs moving faster than he had intended. His mind kept racing, too, glancing over his shoulder every few steps, half-expecting to see something—anything—following him. The adrenaline in his veins urged him to keep moving, to not look back, and to not slow down. He wasn't sure if it was fear or sheer instinct driving him, but he couldn't shake the feeling that something was still out there.

By the time Doug reached the front door of his house, his chest was heaving with exertion, his breath shallow and ragged. Janet was standing at the door, a concerned expression on her face.

"I was just about ready to go looking for you... Why are you panting so hard?" she asked, her tone direct and no-nonsense.

Doug barely noticed her words. He could see the concern in her eyes, though, and it only added to the unease gnawing at him. Janet was the practical type—no small talk, no games. If she was asking questions, it meant she was worried. She paused, her gaze sweeping over him. It only took a moment for her to notice how pale his face had become, the almost translucent quality to his skin.

She stepped closer, her eyes narrowing. "Doug, are you okay? You don't look well," she said, her voice softening with concern.

Doug was too tired to offer an explanation right away. He leaned against the doorframe, trying to steady his breathing, but the pounding in his chest wasn't just from running. He could feel his heart racing from something deeper. He tried to force a smile, but it didn't reach his eyes.

Janet's eyes narrowed further as she looked at him, noticing his discomfort. She knew all too well the toll Doug's migraines could take on him—how they would leave him laid out on the ground, unable to function. If he had fallen out there, she thought, he would have had to lie down... and I would have to call for help. She knew she couldn't lift him on her own if he collapsed again.

"Doug," she began softly, "what happened out there?"

But Doug didn't have an answer. He was still too shaken, still too uncertain of what had really happened, and still too terrified to admit that he might not be alone—whether in the woods or in his mind.

Doug understood that Janet would never fully believe the strange, terrifying experience he'd just had, especially since he still wasn't sure himself what had really happened. So, he settled for a more mundane explanation, telling her he had simply decided to jog back home. Janet's brow furrowed slightly as she listened, the skepticism clear in her eyes. She knew there was more to the story, but she didn't press him further. Instead, she gave a small nod, her gaze softening as she closed the door behind him.

"You better sit down for a while," she said firmly, gesturing toward a chair. Her voice, though calm, carried an undercurrent of concern as she watched him carefully.

Doug hesitated for a moment, his legs still shaky from the unsettling run back, but he didn't argue. His body ached from the adrenaline and tension, and his mind was too exhausted to think clearly. He slowly made his way to the chair, sinking into it with a heavy sigh. Janet's concern was palpable, but so was the quiet insistence in her voice—she knew him well enough to sense when something was off.

The weeks that followed were difficult for Doug. He found himself constantly on edge, as if he were waiting for something to happen—though he wasn't sure exactly what. Any unexpected noise, or a hand placed on his shoulder from behind, would send his heart racing, nearly causing him to jump out of his skin. He tried to go on with his life as best as he could, but the strange events in the woods haunted him. The terror he'd felt lingered in his mind, a shadow that he couldn't shake. He wanted to tell someone about what had happened, but he knew no one would believe him. They would think he was crazy, and that fear kept him silent.

For months, Doug kept the experience to himself. He tried to push it to the back of his mind, but it never truly left. It wasn't until one ordinary afternoon at work that something triggered the memory again. Doug was sitting at his desk, dictating a letter to his secretary, Tina, when his boss walked in unexpectedly. Without warning, he dropped a folder on the floor, the sound of it hitting the ground sharp and loud. Tina jerked in her seat, her body reacting as if she had been shocked by an electric current. Her reaction was so intense that Doug couldn't help but notice. His boss, a man of few words, simply smiled, muttered an apology, and picked up the folder before handing it to Doug and leaving without another word.

Doug raised an eyebrow, watching Tina as she tried to calm herself. "A little jumpy, aren't we?" he asked, a teasing smile on his face.

Tina, still rattled, nodded slightly. "Ah... a little," she said, her voice unsure. She wanted to end the conversation right there, but Doug's gaze lingered on her, and she could tell by the look in his eyes that he wasn't going to let it slide. He was curious, and he wasn't going to be satisfied with a vague response.

Tina hesitated. Should I tell him? Or not? she thought. She had no idea how Doug would react if she shared her story with him. She had barely told anyone, and even then, only a select few knew about the strange experiences that had been haunting her for weeks.

Doug, sensing her reluctance, pressed on. "Am I working you too hard?" he asked with a smile, trying to keep the mood light. He knew he had been asking her to stay late a lot recently, working overtime to help him secure a contract that could mean a promotion or raise for both of them. He didn't want her to feel overburdened.

Tina shook her head quickly. "No, it's nothing like that," she said, her voice wavering slightly. She didn't want to go into detail, not yet. The truth was, she had been dealing with something unsettling herself, and she wasn't sure how Doug would react if she told him. He might think I need to see a professional, she thought, her mind racing. But what if he understood? What if he had experienced something similar?

"Well, go ahead," Doug said, his voice gentle but encouraging. "Maybe it'll help to get it out in the open. Unless, of course, it's too personal." He gave her a reassuring smile, sensing she was holding something back.

Tina hesitated for a moment, feeling the weight of the decision. She knew she shouldn't say anything—she wasn't one to open up easily—but once she started, the words began tumbling out faster than she could control. She had always been a shy woman, not the type to share personal matters with just anyone. But Doug had been kind, and she needed someone to hear her, to understand.

"Well," she began, taking a deep breath, "it all started one of those nights I worked late for you." She knew she probably shouldn't say anything, but something inside her compelled her to speak. Taking off her glasses, she set them down on Doug's desk, the action almost symbolic as she prepared to lay bare the strange, unsettling experience that had been tormenting her. "I don't know if you'll believe me, but I have to tell someone."

Doug listened attentively; his expression curious but patient. Tina could see the skepticism in his eyes, but he didn't interrupt, and that gave her the courage to continue.

"I know this is going to sound... well, shall we say, out of this world? Or maybe even ridiculous," Tina continued, her voice trembling slightly. "But I want you to know I'm not making any of this up." She stopped, her hands clenched tightly in her lap. She was shaking, but she pressed on. If she didn't talk about it, she was afraid she'd lose her mind.

"I left here around eight o'clock. It was already dark by then," she explained. "I live just across the park in that new high-rise. Normally, I'd take a cab because of the cold, but that night it was pretty nice out—just before we got that cold snap. So, I decided to walk."

Tina placed her notepad on Doug's desk, her hands slightly unsteady as she continued. "I stayed on the lighted sidewalk, the one that runs through the park. It's well-lit, except for a few trees here and there that block the streetlamps. As I was walking, I thought I heard something behind me. I turned around, but there was no one there. I could see all the way back to the building."

Her voice faltered, and she glanced down, as if recalling the moment. "I kept walking, and that's when it started feeling... strange. It seemed like whatever it was, it was getting closer. Every so often, I'd glance back and catch a glimpse of it in the corner of my eye, but I never really saw it—at least, not clearly. You know what I mean?"

Doug's face softened as he nodded, his mind whirring as he thought about her words. "Yes. I do," he said quietly, realizing just how familiar her story sounded. The hairs on the back of his neck stood up as the echoes of his own strange experience came rushing back. Tina hadn't finished yet, but Doug had a sinking feeling that he was hearing the beginning of a much bigger story—one that he wasn't sure he was ready to hear, but one that he also couldn't ignore.

"You do?" Tina asked, her voice laced with surprise and bewilderment.

"Yes," Doug replied with a nod, his tone steady but reflective. "I'll explain later. Please, go on. I want to hear more."

Tina hesitated for a moment, her brows furrowed as she studied Doug's face, searching for sincerity. Satisfied with his earnestness, she continued. "Well, I was about halfway across the park when I suddenly felt something bite my leg. At first, I thought it might've been a stray dog. The pain was sharp, and when I tried to see what had bitten me, I lost my balance and tumbled to the ground."

Doug leaned forward; his attention unwavering as Tina recounted her experience.

"I hit the pavement hard," she said, wincing at the memory. "Whatever it was released its grip, and I managed to look up. I was trying to figure out what had attacked me so I could crawl away, but then I saw it. Teeth—large, gleaming teeth—sinking into my leg again."

She swallowed hard, her hands clutching at the fabric of her skirt as she spoke. "I panicked and swung my purse at it. The pain was blinding, and my swing didn't even connect. It went right through... like whatever it was wasn't entirely there. Like it was some kind of ghost or hallucination."

Doug felt a chill run down his spine but stayed silent, allowing her to continue.

"The pain was too much," Tina said softly. "I blacked out right there on the sidewalk. I don't know how long I was unconscious. When I woke up, it was freezing, and I was lying there alone. My first instinct was to check my legs. I pulled my skirt down and looked, expecting the worst—torn fabric, blood, bite marks—but there was nothing. No rips, no wounds, not even scratches. Just a couple of small bruises from the fall."

Her voice faltered, and she looked up at Doug, her expression torn between disbelief and fear. "It was like... like it had never happened. Like it was all just some terrible nightmare."

Doug exhaled slowly, processing what he'd just heard. Tina's account mirrored his own experience in eerie, unsettling ways. The same confusion, the same inexplicable pain, and the same lack of evidence afterward. He rubbed the back of his neck, deciding how best to respond without alarming her or sounding dismissive.

"Tina," he began carefully, "what you've just described... it's almost identical to something that happened to me."

Her eyes widened, and she leaned forward. "What do you mean? When?"

Doug paused, collecting his thoughts. "A couple of months ago. I had a strange encounter—if you can even call it that—out in the woods. There was something there, something I couldn't see clearly, but I felt it. It... well, it attacked me. Or at least, I thought it did. But when it was over, there was nothing. No scratches, no tears in my clothes, no proof that it even happened."

Tina listened intently; her hands pressed against her mouth in shock. When Doug finished recounting his experience, the two sat in silence, staring at each other as they grappled with the surreal similarities.

Finally, Doug broke the silence. "There's something else," he said cautiously. "I've been seeing Dr. Wilson for my migraines. Last time I visited him—"

"Wait," Tina interrupted, her eyes narrowing. "Dr. Wilson? I've been seeing him too. For migraines. And... the last time I saw him; he gave me this trial medication. A liquid. He told me to take it with an aspirin."

Doug froze, his mind racing. "That's exactly what he told me." The realization hit them both like a freight train.

A heavy silence fell over the room again, the weight of their shared experiences pressing down on them. Finally, Doug spoke, his voice steady but tinged with apprehension. "Tina, I think we need to find out exactly what's going on. And I think it starts with Dr. Wilson."

"We're both seeing the same doctor who gave us the same medication?" Doug leaned forward, his eyes narrowing in thought. "He gave me an eight-ounce bottle of some thick, nasty-looking liquid and told me to take it with an aspirin too."

Tina nodded, her expression a mix of curiosity and unease. Doug began recounting how he first came across Dr. Wilson. "I was having one of my worst migraines—the kind where it feels like your skull's being drilled into. My eyes were watering so badly I could barely see straight. I was sitting at the kitchen table, trying to ride it out, when I grabbed the newspaper for distraction. At some point, when the pain eased enough for me to focus, I noticed this ad staring back at me: 'Having migraines? Can't find relief? Willing to try new medication guaranteed to relieve your pain? Come to my office and feel relieved.'"

Tina's eyes widened. "Me too," she said, her voice rising slightly. "I saw the same ad in the paper. I was in so much pain, I would've done anything to stop it."

Doug leaned back in his chair. "That's what I thought too. Desperate times and all."

"There's one weird thing about it, though," Tina added hesitantly.

Doug looked up. "What's that?"

"When I tried to find the ad again later, it wasn't there. I combed through every section of the paper but nothing. If I hadn't written down the address, I would've thought I imagined the whole thing."

Doug's face stiffened as he processed her words. "I didn't go back to check the ad," he said, "but now that you mention it, that does sound... odd."

The room grew quiet for a moment as both of them reached instinctively for their medication bottles. Tina pulled hers from her purse, while Doug retrieved his from his desk drawer. They placed them side by side on the desk, comparing the labels. Identical. The same murky liquid, the same prescription, and the same doctor.

"He said it was experimental," Tina remarked, inspecting her bottle. "And it did work on the migraine. That part's true."

Doug nodded slowly, his mind racing. "But what about these side effects?"

They sat in silence for a moment, the implications of their shared experience weighing heavily between them.

Finally, Doug broke the tension. "How about this—we take a day off and go see Dr. Wilson together. Confront him. Find out what's really going on with this medication."

Tina hesitated, then gave a resolute nod. "That's a good idea. Maybe he can explain these... side effects. Or at least give us some answers."

Doug glanced at the bottles one last time, a chill creeping up his spine. "Let's hope he has them," he muttered.

Kyle Thomas stepped out of his house, a bag of trash in hand, heading for the curb where the weekly pickup would soon make its rounds. As he set the bag down, a sudden, sharp pain shot through his temple like a lightning bolt.

"Not another migraine," he groaned, clutching his head with one hand while leaning against the trash container with the other. His vision blurred, and the pounding in his skull grew unbearable. Before he could steady himself, his knees buckled, and he collapsed onto the grass at the edge of his yard.

Moments later, his neighbor, Greg, who had been out watering his plants, noticed Kyle on the ground and rushed over. "Hey, Kyle! You okay, buddy?" Greg knelt beside him; his voice filled with concern. He gently shook Kyle's shoulder but quickly realized his neighbor was unconscious.

Looking around, Greg called out to another neighbor, "Someone get help! Call 911!" But before the others could react, Kyle let out a low groan, his hand twitching slightly as he began to stir.

Kyle's eyelids fluttered open, and he mumbled incoherently at first. Struggling to sit up, he finally managed to speak. "I'm fine. Just got a little dizzy, that's all," he muttered, rubbing his head and trying to steady himself.

Greg frowned, unconvinced. "You sure? You were out cold for a minute there."

Kyle nodded weakly, attempting to wave off the concern. "Yeah, I'm okay now. Thanks for the help, though."

Reluctantly, Greg offered a hand to help Kyle to his feet. With effort, Kyle stood, swaying slightly before regaining his balance. As he began to make his way back to the house, the throbbing pain that had overwhelmed him earlier seemed to have vanished.

Pausing at the steps of his deck, Kyle realized something strange. The debilitating migraine that had struck him so suddenly—the one that had caused his collapse—was completely gone. No lingering ache, no tension in his temples. Nothing.

"That's odd," he murmured to himself, glancing back at Greg, who was still watching him with a wary expression. Kyle offered a thumbs-up and a faint smile to reassure his neighbor before heading inside, his mind racing with questions about the mysterious turn of events.

Kyle knew he needed to reach out to Doug immediately and share the bizarre incident he had experienced, even if there was a chance that Doug might dismiss it as unbelievable. After all, Doug was the one who had originally recommended Dr. Wilson to him, making him a key part of this strange situation.

Grabbing his phone, Kyle dialed Doug's number, mentally preparing himself to recount the unsettling details of what had transpired. When Doug answered, Kyle wasted no time explaining the events, ensuring he didn't leave out any significant details. He described the inexplicable appearance of the creature, the sharp pain, and the mysterious disappearance of all evidence of the attack. Doug listened carefully, and while his tone was calm, there was a hint of recognition in his voice.

"Yeah, we know," Doug finally responded, his words both surprising and intriguing. "My secretary, Tina, experienced something similar. It sounds like we might all be dealing with the same issue. She and I were already planning to visit Dr. Wilson's office this Friday to look into this further. It would be a good idea if you joined us. Maybe we can figure out what's going on."

The call ended quickly, but it left Kyle with a mix of relief and curiosity. While he was unsettled by the realization that others had shared similar experiences, he felt reassured that he wasn't alone in facing this mystery. Meeting up with Doug and Tina to confront Dr. Wilson seemed like the logical next step in uncovering the truth behind these perplexing events.

That Friday, Doug, Tina, and Kyle arrived at the address where Dr. Wilson's office was supposed to be located, the same place where each of them had previously received the mysterious liquid medication prescribed for their migraines. However, as they stood in front of the building, their confusion grew.

What they expected to be a functioning medical office turned out to be nothing more than an abandoned structure. The building appeared to have been vacant for a significant amount of time, with signs of neglect evident in the cracked and crumbling exterior. Weeds pushed through the broken pavement surrounding the site, and windows were either shattered or boarded up, giving the entire scene an eerie, desolate feel.

The stark contrast between their memories of a professional medical establishment and the current state of the property left them questioning everything. How could a place they had all visited so recently now look as though it had been deserted for years? The realization hit hard, and the three of them exchanged puzzled glances, struggling to make sense of what they were seeing.

The three of them stood in disbelief, staring at the crumbling façade of the building. The address was unmistakable—etched into the brick beside a rusted metal door—but the scene before them was anything but what they remembered.

"This can't be right," Doug muttered, frowning as he took a cautious step forward. "I was just here a couple of weeks ago. It was a clean, modern office. There were people in the waiting room. Tina, you were here too, right?"

Tina nodded, clutching her coat tighter around her as if warding off a sudden chill. "Yes. It was pristine. A receptionist, bright lights, everything. This place looks like it's been abandoned for decades."

Kyle tilted his head, scanning the structure. "I came here just a few days ago. The door was functional, there were signs... This is surreal."

Doug tried the door, but it wouldn't budge. The handle was rusted solid, as if untouched for years. He rattled it once more, then stepped back in frustration. "Okay, this is insane."

"Wait a second," Kyle said, pointing to a broken window near the corner of the building. "If this place is abandoned, maybe we can get inside and look around. There might be something that explains what's going on."

Tina hesitated, glancing between them. "You're suggesting we break into a condemned building? That's how horror movies start, you know."

Doug raised an eyebrow. "After what we've all experienced, I'd say we're already in one."

Reluctantly, the three made their way to the window. Kyle hoisted himself through first, landing with a crunch on shattered glass and debris. "Be careful," he said, helping Tina and Doug climb inside.

The interior was dark and smelled of mildew. Dust coated every surface, and broken furniture lay scattered across the floor. Cobwebs hung from the ceiling, and faint beams of sunlight filtered through cracks in the walls. It was a stark contrast to the well-lit, professional office they all remembered.

"This... doesn't make sense," Tina whispered, her voice echoing in the empty space.

Doug shone the flashlight on his phone across the room, revealing a desk. It was the only intact piece of furniture, sitting oddly pristine in the otherwise decrepit space. On it lay a folder, slightly yellowed but otherwise untouched by the decay around it.

"Look at this," Doug said, picking up the folder. Inside were patient records—his, Tina's, and Kyle's. Their names, addresses, and the same prescription written in Dr. Wilson's handwriting.

Tina gasped. "How is this even here?"

Kyle clenched his fists. "This is getting weirder by the second. Who is this guy? And why did he give us that medication?"

As they flipped through the records, they found something chilling. A handwritten note at the back of the folder read:

"Experiment successful. Migraines eliminated. Side effects manageable. Subjects unaware of secondary purpose."

The three of them exchanged nervous glances, the weight of the words sinking in.

"What secondary purpose?" Tina asked, her voice trembling.

Doug shook his head. "I don't know... but I think we've been part of something a lot bigger than we realized."

Suddenly, a loud creak echoed through the building. They froze, staring at the doorway as footsteps began to approach from the hall.

As the three of them stood there, a man walked over. "You guys looking to buy this old building? My name is Robert, Bob for short," he also extended his hand to shake.

Doug began, while scratching his head. "I was here a few weeks ago and it was an office."

Bob chuckled, "Not here. This place has been vacant for around fourteen years. In fact, I think the city condemned it."

"I checked and rechecked the address," Tina told Bob. "It is the same as what I wrote down."

"Apparently, you wrote it down wrong, missy," replied Bob.

After a few apologies the three of them convinced Bob to let them outside. Glad to be rid of them. Bob walked away shaking his head. "Idiots," he mumbled.

"I wonder what the ingredients were for this," remarked Tina, as she held up the bottle her medicine had been in.

"Well, it's empty," said Kyle, as he looked at Tina's bottle.

Doug pulled his medicine bottle out as well; it too was empty. "What's going on? I should have had a half bottle left." he said

Kyle reached in his backpack and pulled out his medicine bottle. "Mine is empty too".

As they stood in the cold, the questions seemed to multiply faster than the answers. Tina twisted the empty bottle in her hands, staring at it as if it might hold some clue. "If everything else disappeared—the office, the doctor, even the supposed creatures—why are these still here? And why are they empty now?"

Doug, still clutching his own bottle, gave a weak laugh. "You're right. This doesn't make sense. If this was just a hallucination, how did we all have the same experience? And these bottles… they're the only physical evidence we have that any of it happened."

Kyle shook his head, running a hand through his hair. "The migraines are gone, but at what cost? What if those hallucinations—or whatever they were—weren't just some side affect, what if we were part of something bigger? An experiment, like that note in the folder said."

Tina's gaze darted back to the crumbling building. "And if this place has been abandoned for over a decade, where the hell were we? Who was Dr. Wilson?"

Doug looked down at the bottle in his hand, his jaw tightening. "We need to find out. There has to be a way to figure out who this guy really is and what he's been doing. If this is some underground experiment, he didn't just vanish into thin air."

"But how?" asked Kyle. "We don't even know if that was his real name. The building doesn't exist, and the only things we have are these stupid bottles."

Tina's expression hardened. "Maybe the bottles are the key. Someone manufactured this stuff. There might be a lab, a company, or some traceable mark on them. And I'm not just going to sit here and let this go. Whatever happened to us, we deserve to know."

Doug nodded, his resolve matching hers. "Let's take these bottles to a lab, see if they can analyze any residue. Maybe they can tell us what was in the liquid—or at least point us in a direction."

Kyle exhaled deeply. "This is starting to feel like something out of a bad sci-fi movie."

"Maybe," Doug said, sliding the bottle back into his pocket. "But it's our lives. And if someone's been messing with us, they're going to regret it."

The three of them exchanged determined looks. Whatever had happened to them—whether it was real, a shared hallucination, or something even stranger—they were going to find answers. Together.

Them

Many of the stories' people write are works of pure fiction—crafted from their imagination, often sprung from nowhere, and eventually turned into major motion pictures or best-selling books. The power of the imagination is truly remarkable, wouldn't you agree?

Well, I find myself in a somewhat similar position. The tale I am about to share is, in part, based on actual events, though with a healthy dose of imagination thrown in to fill in the gaps. I'm confident that as you read it, you'll come to see the reality in it. Now, without further delay, let's dive into the action.

It all began roughly two years ago. On this particular evening, I was sitting comfortably in my favorite chair—the one that's so irresistibly cozy that it's become the unwritten rule of the house: no one, especially the children, dares to sit in it when I want to unwind and watch a good show on television. My wife was in the kitchen, busy preparing dinner, and I could hear her muttering about how she never got to watch the beginning of any show because I was always so engrossed in whatever I was watching.

As I settled into my chair, fully immersed in the movie, I caught a glimpse of something moving quickly across the floor from the corner of my eye. Initially, I thought it might be a mouse, or worse, one of those dreaded wolf spiders I can't stand. I glanced in the direction of the movement but saw nothing there. Shrugging it off, I resumed my seat and continued watching the film, like any committed science fiction fan would.

Still, a lingering sense of unease caused me to glance towards the area periodically. Each time, I would lower my feet back to the floor, trying to convince myself that I had simply imagined the movement. Eventually, I put the matter out of my mind. At that moment, it was just a brief, unremarkable experience—one that seemed insignificant in the grand scheme of things.

Before I continue, let me ask you something: Have you ever been deeply focused on something and then, out of the corner of your eye, thought you saw something moving? Yet, when you looked directly, there was nothing there? It's strange how our minds can play tricks on us, isn't it?

Although I started this story with a bit of lightheartedness, my next encounter wasn't nearly as amusing. This time, the events unfolded about two weeks later. The situation was eerily similar to the first, except this time my wife had gone to town to pick up a missing ingredient for a recipe she was making. Knowing she'd be gone for some time (a scenario that, for some reason, always seems to involve her coming home with more than she went for), I settled into my chair, feeling confident I could enjoy some uninterrupted peace and quiet.

I hadn't been sitting for long before I saw something dart across the floor between the television and the couch. The sight was so quick that I barely had time to react. Instinctively, I pulled my feet up onto the footstool to protect them, but the discomfort in my ankle was unbearable. I had a sinking feeling—perhaps one of those dreaded wolf spiders had latched onto my leg. I quickly jumped out of my chair, expecting to find a spider, only to discover something far more terrifying.

What I saw next was beyond anything I could have imagined. There, attached to my ankle, was a small, hairy creature, its fangs deeply embedded in my skin. Blood was running down my leg, pooling onto the footstool. In a panic, I grabbed my sock and pressed it against the wound, trying to stem the flow, but my vision was beginning to blur, and I felt lightheaded. I collapsed back into the chair, desperately trying to make sense of what I was seeing.

The creature was unlike anything I had ever encountered in my life. It was small—no more than six inches in diameter—with a body covered in thick, coarse hair. It had no tail, just two spindly legs with long claws that seemed to cling to my ankle. The creature's mouth was wide open, revealing jagged teeth that were nearly two inches long—far too large for its size. Above its fangs were two eyes, bloodshot and gleaming with an unsettling, predatory look. It was as if it used its mouth like an additional set of legs, gripping my ankle with terrifying strength.

In an attempt to defend myself, I grabbed a nearby book from the shelf and swung it toward the creature. But when the book made contact, there was no resistance—no impact, nothing. The creature seemed to be made of air, passing right through the book without a trace. Still, it clung to my ankle, its grip tightening with each passing moment.

In a panic, I tried to stand, hoping to run for help, but the moment I rose from the chair, the world began to spin. My vision went gray, then black, and I collapsed, losing consciousness as I fell to the floor.

The next thing I remember was waking up to the sound of my wife's voice. She was kneeling beside me, concern etched on her face. "Are you okay?" she asked.

I groggily glanced at my ankle and the footstool. "No, I'm not okay. Look at my ankle—and the blood on the footstool!" I responded.

She looked at my ankle, then at the footstool, but seemed confused. "What blood? What are you talking about?"

I was in a daze. My ankle looked perfectly normal. There were no bite marks, no blood. Nothing at all.

"I don't understand," I said, my voice filled with confusion. I pulled up my pant leg, but there was no sign of the injury I had felt moments earlier. The wound, the blood—it was all gone.

With a bemused expression, my wife shook her head. "I think I understand. You've been watching too many of those creepy movies. You probably just fell asleep and had a nightmare."

Her words hung in the air, but I couldn't shake the feeling that something wasn't right. What had happened? What was real, and what had been a product of my imagination?

I may never know the answer, but I can tell you this: The mind is a powerful thing—and sometimes, reality and imagination can blur in ways we don't fully understand.

I began to contradict my wife's words, but something held me back. I knew better than to challenge her in this moment. With a knowing shake of her head, she stood up and returned to the kitchen to finish putting away her groceries. My wife, a kind and understanding woman, often indulged my eccentricities, but there were times when she openly questioned my sanity. We had been married for several years, and despite my quirks, we had built a life of happiness together. Yet, on occasion, she would express concern, wondering if perhaps I was losing touch with reality.

As she disappeared into the kitchen, I sank deeper into my chair, no longer interested in the television. I turned my gaze to the floor, lost in thought. That was my second encounter with the creatures. The first had been fleeting, just a brief moment where I glimpsed them, and then they vanished as quickly as they had appeared. But what I was experiencing now, I couldn't ignore. My mind was still reeling from what had happened, and it left me shaken.

A few weeks had passed since that initial unsettling encounter, and for the most part, I had managed to push it from my mind. But that nagging sense of unease still lingered at the back of my thoughts. From time to time, I would catch myself glancing nervously at the periphery of my vision, hoping not to see movement where there was none. It had been six months since my last experience with these creatures, and I had almost convinced myself that it had all been a figment of my imagination. But deep down, I knew something was off, even if I couldn't explain it.

It was a quiet evening when the third encounter occurred. My wife, who was working late, had called to let me know she would be at the office for a couple more hours. She needed to prepare reports for a meeting the following day, and I had no problem with that. There was a movie I had been eagerly waiting for all week—another sci-fi film, of course. I flopped down into my chair, grabbed the remote, and settled in for an evening of entertainment. The movie began, its opening scenes setting the stage for a thrilling ride. But before I could fully immerse myself in the film, I saw something that immediately pulled me out of my trance.

From the left side of the television screen, something small and fast darted across the floor. Then another appeared on the right side. One came out from behind the couch, and another emerged from under the bookshelf. My heart began to race. "No!" I shouted at the screen, though I knew it wouldn't help. "You're not real!"

But they didn't vanish. They didn't disappear. I squeezed my eyes shut, hoping to wish them away, but when I opened them again, they were still there, moving with unnatural speed. "My God, they're everywhere!" I yelled, my voice rising in panic. The creatures just kept coming, one after another. I counted at least eight or nine of them before my sense of disbelief finally gave way to fear.

Desperate, I bolted from my chair and made my way toward the kitchen. I needed something to defend myself. Grabbing the butcher knife from the counter, I clutched it tightly, preparing for whatever was about to happen next. At that moment, I thought I might confront my wife and ask her whether she thought I was losing my mind. But before I could even get a grip on the situation, the creatures attacked.

They swarmed around my ankles, their claws digging into my skin, and with terrifying strength, they forced me to the ground. The knife slipped from my hand, skidding across the tiled floor. I tried to reach for it, stretching my arm out, but it was just out of my grasp. I dug my fingers into the cold floor, trying to pull my body closer to the knife, but it was useless. The creatures were far stronger than I could ever be.

Then, to my horror, one of them sank its fangs deep into my scalp, jerking my head backward. Before I could react, two others scurried across the floor and grabbed the knife with their teeth. They raced back toward me, aiming for my exposed throat. The slice was swift and brutal. Blood sprayed across the room, pooling on the floor, and I heard a gurgling sound as I tried to breathe, but the air was blocked. The pain in my left hand became unbearable. The fingers I had stretched out to grab the knife were cut to the bone, and my wedding band was gone—ripped off my finger by the vicious creatures.

At that point, I thought I was dead. The world faded to black. When I finally regained consciousness, I was lying on the kitchen floor, my head resting in my wife's lap. She was slapping my face, trying to rouse me. Her eyes were filled with tears as she spoke, but her words didn't fully register in my dazed state. She later told me that when she found me, she thought I was dead. She said she had never seen me in such a state, and she feared I had gone over the edge mentally. As I began to stir, I mumbled incoherently, talking about the creatures that had attacked me.

Once again, I checked my body for any signs of injury. There were no scratches, no bite marks, and—surprisingly—my wedding band was still on my finger. Everything seemed normal, and yet, I knew what had happened. It had been real. I wasn't imagining it.

My wife, though concerned, insisted I see a doctor. After much discussion, I reluctantly agreed. We scheduled an appointment for the following week, though part of me wasn't sure what a doctor could do about something so... unbelievable.

Before I could even make it to the doctor, the creatures attacked again. This time, my wife was downstairs, doing laundry. I was in the bathroom, shaving, when I thought I saw something move behind the shower curtain. I paused, wondering if I was imagining things. My wife had been convincing me that these creatures were merely a product of my overactive imagination. She believed they weren't real, that my mind was playing tricks on me, which was why she insisted I see a doctor. I tried to ignore the feeling that something was there. But deep down, I knew better.

I finished shaving, feeling a sense of relief as the task came to an end. I set my razor down and, after removing my clothes, I turned on the shower. However, as the water began to run, I immediately noticed a strange sound, one that was not typical for my usual shower routine. The sound was subtle at first, but it quickly caught my attention. I pulled back the shower curtain, expecting to find perhaps a forgotten item or an object my wife had left in the tub. But instead, I was met with a much more unsettling sight.

There, in the tub, was one of them. It was unmistakable. My blood ran cold. Without thinking, I tried to jump back out of the bathroom, hoping to distance myself from whatever nightmare was unfolding before me. But as I attempted to retreat, several more of the creatures quickly scurried up my back, their claws digging into my skin, and in an instant, I was thrust forward, crashing into the tub. I instinctively grabbed the shower curtain on the way down, desperately trying to steady myself, but the water, despite its usual calming presence, seemed to have no effect on the creatures. They were relentless.

For what felt like an eternity, I struggled to free myself, but each time I knocked one of the creatures away, another seemed to take its place. Their movements were fast, almost supernatural, and their grip was unnaturally strong. The pain from their bites was excruciating, and soon the once-clear water in the tub began to turn a deep red, stained by the blood that poured from my wounds. Despite my efforts to resist, I felt my strength waning. I knew I could no longer fight them off. I was exhausted, both physically and mentally, and I realized in that moment that they would not relent until they had their fill.

As the creatures continued their assault, I became aware that my wife was nearby. She had, in fact, anticipated that I would finish shaving soon and had undressed outside the bathroom in preparation to join me in the shower. But as soon as she opened the door and saw the scene before her, she let out a scream that pierced the air, a scream so loud and filled with terror that it threw me into a panic. My first thought was that she, too, was being attacked. *My God*, the creatures must be real. They were attacking her as well!

I tried to reach out to her, desperate to help, but the pain was overwhelming. The blood loss was too much, and I succumbed to unconsciousness once more.

When I regained consciousness, I found myself straddling the edge of the bathtub, my body aching and uncomfortable. My immediate concern was for my wife. I looked around the bathroom, but she wasn't there. Panic gripped me, and I rushed to the door, where I found her lying motionless on the floor in the hallway just outside. She was curled up in a fetal position, her body limp, but there wasn't a mark on her. Despite this, I could see that she had been deeply affected. I recalled with horrifying clarity the image of blood running down her chest, staining her skin as one of the creatures had bitten into her cheek. I tried to shake the memory, but it lingered, too vivid to ignore.

I quickly gathered her up in my arms and carried her to the bedroom. Carefully, I laid her down on the bed, brushing the tangled strands of her red hair away from her face. I covered her with a sheet, trying to comfort her, though I wasn't sure if I was truly comforting her or myself. After a moment, I returned to the bathroom, but as I stood in the doorway, I surveyed the room. It looked entirely normal, almost too normal. There was nothing out of place, no sign of the horrors I had just endured. With a deep breath, I grabbed a washcloth and rinsed it under cold water, squeezing out the excess before returning to my wife's side.

I gently cradled her head in my hands, wiping her face with the cool cloth in an attempt to bring her back to consciousness. When her eyes finally fluttered open, I could see the sheer terror reflected in them. The look on her face was enough to terrify anyone, and in that moment, I realized just how deeply this had affected her. I held her close, trying to reassure her, though deep down I knew that nothing was truly all right. Her body was trembling, and I could feel her entire form shaking with fear and confusion.

With great care, I helped her get dressed and guided her to the car. She didn't say much as we drove, and I wasn't sure what to say either. When we arrived at the hospital, I found myself at a loss for words. How could I explain to the doctors what had happened? What could I possibly say that would make them believe such an unbelievable story? In the end, I simply told them she had passed out, though I knew they didn't buy it. How could they? How could anyone believe that *they* were real?

I was sure the doctors didn't believe a word of it, but who could blame them? After all, *have you ever seen them*? Have you ever seen the creatures that haunt the edges of your vision, lurking just beyond what the eye can fully comprehend? I doubt it. But that doesn't mean they're not out there—*or maybe they're already right here with you.* Look around. Do you see anything? Wait... what was that movement behind you?

As for my wife, she is physically okay, but she hasn't been the same since that night. She still glances nervously at any small movement, even something as simple as the wind rustling the leaves outside. She always wonders—could they be hidden among the leaves, waiting for the perfect moment to strike? Sometimes, I wonder too. After all, they may not be far at all. They could be lurking in the outermost edges of your vision, just to the right, or to the left. Perhaps you'll see them, just like I do. Or maybe... you'll never know until it's too late.

Enhanced Feelings

The kitchen, which had been decorated with every modern convenience that one could imagine was now, being redecorated with a brilliant red. Let's call it a warm human tint.

The sounds coming from the twisting of the knife in the woman's side was like the breaking of a chicken's breast as it was being prepared for the frying pan.

Everything was happening in slow motion; the weapon being slowly drawn from its victim as the body slithered to the floor. The lifeless form was now lying in its own life-giving substance. It was over, she would never gripe at him again!

It had all started that morning. Gerald had gone to the local pawn shop to find something for his wife for her birthday. He figured the pawn shop could save him some money since they had been on a tight budget. When he returned home and gave his wife the toaster oven he had found (she had said she wished she had had one for a long time), she started bitching at him for spending so much money. Even though he had only spent half the price it would have cost at the local discount store.

Gerald had also spent one dollar on a necklace that caught his eye. It was circular with a figure of someone's head in the middle. What had attracted Gerald to this piece of jewelry was the figure. Even though it was rough, it kind of resembled him!

Gerald was a kind of shy person, never said too much to anyone, especially his wife. He was an office worker with enough time to retire. He considered it several times
but didn't want to be home with his nagging wife every day. She was a couple inches shorter than him and about fifty pounds lighter. He decided, enough was enough. He just couldn't take it anymore. He had grabbed the knife off the counter and plunged it in her side. No more nagging, he thought.

After he had killed his wife, he called the police and turned himself in. They found him kneeling beside her weeping. He hated her nagging but at the same time he loved her. Regretting what he had done, he went with the police, to face his punishment. Since he pleaded guilty, the judgment came quickly. He was found guilty and sentenced to life in prison.

The necklace was removed and turned in when he went to the police station. He didn't have a chance to give it to her and was clinging to it when the police arrived. They told him that they would keep it for him and send it to his next of kin which was his sister.

The necklace was never sent to his sister. It had been stolen by Office Robert Ford, the policeman that had arrested him. He had a brother that was having a birthday coming up soon and figured it would be a cheap present to give him. Had he read the inscription on the back, he might have changed his mind even though he thought the figure resembled his brother.

Once Thomas Ford had received the medallion from his brother, he turned it over and read the inscription on the back: "Beware of the unseen force"

"What does this mean? Where did you get it? Is this some kind of joke?" asked Thomas.

"Hey! I don't know what it means, and don't worry about where I got it. I thought it looked a lot like you so I got it for ya, "replied Bob.

"Thanks, I guess," said his brother.

"Why you jerk. Here I buy you a present and all you do is ask questions about it, "said Bob.

"Look, I'm getting sick and tired of you calling me a jerk every time I ask you a question. Here take this damn thing and stick it where the sun doesn't shine!" replied Thomas.

"Boy, you really are a jerk," repeated Bob.

"That does it!" Thomas reached for the revolver that his brother had been wearing.

Bob always removed the holster when he came into the house at the request of his brother, but not today. Pulling the gun out, he aimed it at Bob's head and squeezed the trigger. There was a loud roar as the gun responded to Thomas's finger. The back of Bob's head flew across the living room, leaving a trail of blood and brains scattered on the carpet. Thomas dropped to the floor on his knees.

"What have I done?" he said as he dropped the revolver on the floor. He didn't know what to do now. Should he run or turn himself in?

Talking to himself, Thomas thought he would wait till morning. "Wait, it is morning, it's three am. I've been sitting here for hours trying to think what to do. Maybe I better I just better get it over with. Maybe I could place the gun so it looks like a suicide. Or maybe I could dump the body somewhere. I could think up a story. No, they wouldn't believe me. I guess it's best to call the police."

When the police arrived, they assessed the situation and immediately arrested him.

Thomas was hauled off to jail. The police lab was called in and they gathered up all the evidence, including the body. When they were finished, they called in a cleaning crew to clean up the mess that had been left.

Emma, one of the cleaning crew, was shampooing the carpet after all the *remains* of Bob's brain had been cleaned up. She pushed the recliner back against the wall and discovered a medallion. Once she held it up, she could see the figure resembled her nephew, Mark.

Emma was very fond of her nephew and she didn't have much money but wanted to give the necklace to him. Didn't think it would harm anything, after all it was on the floor.

Putting it in her pocket she went on cleaning. When done, she headed home to her lonely apartment and sat in her recliner to relax and pulled out the necklace to examine it. Shortly after pulling the locket out, she fell asleep holding it in her hand.

Mark had been a good kid. No matter how good he was though, his parents would come home all different times of the night and start arguing about something. Mark would bite his tongue and try to do what they wanted to keep them quiet. Several times his father would yell and ask him to reply instead of shaking his head. His mother would be too far gone at the bottom of a liquor bottle, and would generally collapse on the couch until the next day. He thought about just leaving and going to his aunt Emma's. Mark really liked his aunt Emma. She was nothing like her sister. Emma was as opposite as night and day.

His mother, Beth, had had it all, the looks, the figure, and the personality that had attracted men. Emma on the other hand was plain, overweight, and she was very shy around the opposite sex.

Emma called Mark on Saturday morning and told him that she had something for him. Mark went right over, as soon as his parents had left for work.

"What cha' got for me aunt Emma?" asked Mark as he sat at the kitchen table drinking a glass of iced tea.

"I know it's not your birthday but I found this necklace with a medallion hanging on it and it seemed to resemble you." she stated

"Oh wow! Hey this is neat! Where did you get it? What does it *say on the* back?"

"I found it at one of the houses that I cleaned, but you don't need to tell anyone. Understand?"

"Right! Thanks a lot!" agreed Mark.

As Emma handed it to him, she remarked "As for the inscription, it says, "Beware of the unseen force". Whatever that means. I have no idea."

After visiting with his aunt for a couple of hours, Mark placed the chain around his neck and looked at his aunt.

"Thanks, aunt Emma", said Mark as he headed for the door.

Being only fifteen, he was not quite old enough to drive, so he got on his bike and headed home. He wanted to get his chores done before his father got home from work. If he didn't, he would probably go into a rage and yell at him again.

It was four o'clock when the boy's parents' old chevy pulled into the driveway. His mother and father got out of the car and headed into the house. His mother handed him a chicken dinner from the local quick food shop.

"We are going to a party tonight. I'll leave some money on the desk. You can take a friend to the movie if you want." With this she and her husband headed for the bedroom to change.

Mark had no intention of going to the show. His favorite show was coming on television tonight and with his parents gone he could watch it, he thought.

At five thirty that evening when the big chevy backed out of the driveway and the couple headed for the big booze party across town. Mark sighed a sigh of relief and went in to fix his chicken and watch TV.

It was one thirty the next morning when the headlights flashed through the front room. There was some cursing as they got out of the car and Mark knew they were falling down drunk again.

"What the hell are you doing up?" asked his father as he took a swing and caught Mark in the corner of his mouth. Before Mark could say anything, his father headed for the bathroom.

"Get me a drink, you little bastard!" said his mother as she plopped down on the edge of the couch cushion which gave way to her unbalanced flop, leaving her lying on the floor passed out with her skirt almost up to her waist.

That did it. Mark walked to the kitchen mumbling so he wouldn't be heard. His parents were disgusting. Tears filled his eyes as he looked around the kitchen in anger. Rage was building in his mind. Something had to be done!

He grabbed the medallion as it swung from his shirt. Then he spotted the gas stove. Through teary eyes, he lifted the stove top and blew out the pilot lights. Then he turned on the burners and heard the gas begin to hiss. He knew that once his father came out of the bathroom, the first thing he would do would be to light up a cigarette, then it would be all over.

Mark's father had passed out after he had thrown up all over the bathroom floor. It was about 15 minutes later when he finally woke up. He was still pretty drunk, and he began yelling for Mark.

Mark never answered his father. He had already gone over to his aunt Emma's and woke her up. After telling her what he had done at his home his aunt wanted to call the authorities, but she also wanted to let it go and see how things went. While she was sitting there comforting her nephew who was sobbing on her shoulder, and trying to make up her mind, she heard an explosion. She didn't have to decide. It was over.

By the time the fire department arrived the whole house was gone due to the explosion. Mark's mother's body had been thrown out into the yard by the explosion. The paramedic pronounced her dead at the scene. There were only the charred remains of his father found where the bathroom had been.

Mark moved in with his aunt and everything seemed to turn out for the best. At least for the time being.

Ever since the report of Gerald killing his wife with the butcher knife, Rick Smears had started investigating the crimes. Rick had been with homicide for seven years and he had a feeling there was something strange about the woman's death.

He had found out from the neighbors that Gerald had really loved his wife even though she did gripe at him a lot. Then there was the case of the policeman that had been shot by his brother for no apparent reason. The two brothers always did everything together. They also fought like brothers do, but enough to kill? That just didn't make sense. Then there was the case of the mother and father killed by the fire.

After thinking this one over he came to a conclusion that this one was completely different. After several weeks of asking questions, he called in his colleague, Randy Morris.

"What do you make of this?" Rick asked, pointing to the blackboard where he had written several names connected with lines, descriptions, and addresses.

"What is this?" asked Randy.

Rick explained "Gerald was arrested by an officer named Robert Ford. Robert Ford was killed by his brother, Thomas. Then there was a woman named Emma, I believe, that cleaned the house after the killing. Wait a minute. Emma had a nephew. The nephew was the one whose parents were killed in that explosion and house fire. There has to be some connection here somewhere, but what?"

"What about the man who killed his wife?" asked Randy.

Rick shrugged his shoulders, turned around and stared at the board once again.

"Ask the kid." suggested Randy.

"Ask what?" Rick responded.

"Well, just talk to him," stated Randy.

"Would you like to go along? Maybe you can figure out something that I may have overlooked."

"Sure, let me give it a try, sounds interesting," replied Randy.

Following the questions from the officers, Mark had turned himself in to the authorities. He admitted to turning on the gas stove and blowing out the pilot lights on his parents' kitchen stove. He went to trial and was found guilty.

He was now spending his time in prison, which may be the rest of his life. His lawyer was trying to get him out on temporary insanity because of the situation, however they tried him as an adult. After Mark had gone through all the process he was taken to his cell. He jumped when they slammed the door to the cell shut and it locked.

"Get used to it kid," replied the guard as he walked away.

George Smith was the guard that had taken Mark's personal items, He had noticed his necklace. "That looks cool," he said as he hung it around his neck without reading the inscription on the back. George was a criminal in his own way. Removing items from inmates that were supposed to be locked up for safe keeping till the inmate either was released or died. Then they would go to the next of kin.

George was doing his four hours in the claims department, then he would do his remaining four hours of his shift watching the prisoners. Looking at his watch, it was now 8 pm, half way through his regular shift.

About 11:30 pm, the yelling started in one of the cells. George knew which one it was and who was in it, Dan.

Dan likes to call himself," Dan the Man". He was yelling that his water wasn't cold enough.

George walked towards Dan's cell, pulling out his club to make Dan understand the rules, as George would put it. George smacked Dan's fingers with the club which made him let out a scream. That wasn't enough. He then unlocked the cell, went inside and started beating Dan.

"Now maybe you will shut up" said George as he raised the club and administered the final blow. The other guards had heard the screaming and came to see the problem.

"George, stop! You are going to kill him!" yelled the approaching guard, trying to pull him away from the now bloody prisoner.

Nothing was working. George kept hitting the lifeless body. Finally, the guard pulled out his taser. He warned George but it was useless. He zapped him and George dropped like a rock.

The third guard removed the probes from George's clothing. He checked for a pulse. "George, has no pulse," he replied. Immediately they tried to revive him, it was too late. They found out later that George had a pacemaker and the sudden jolt had stopped it.

After going through the legal process with his body, they discovered George wanted to be cremated and not buried in an expensive casket.

The funeral home obtained the whereabouts of George's closest relative, a brother. They gave him his possessions that were on the body, including the necklace.

Rick sat at the table, across from Mark. Could you tell me from the start, and please don't leave anything out. No matter how small, please tell me.

Mark told his story, also about the necklace.

"Is that the one you said your aunt found at that house she was cleaning?" asked Rick.

"Yes, is she in trouble?" asked Mark.

"Nah." "Where is the necklace now?" he continued.

"They took it when I came in," answered Mark.

Rick couldn't think of anything else. "That necklace again," he said.

"Oh, ok, thank you," Rick got up and thanked Mark.

He went to the claims room, and asked if he could look through George's belongings.

"Sure, but his brother came and got everything from here," he told Rick. "Now the body, we didn't touch. That would be the funeral home. The stuff we got was from his locker."

Rick thanked him and headed across town to the funeral home. Rick's partner was shifting nervously in the car seat.

"Problem?" asked Rick.

"I just don't like funeral homes," replied Randy.

"You can stay out here. I will be right back," said Rick.

A few minutes later he returned to the car and told Randy, "His brother already picked up his things"

"I did get his address. It's in the next town, called Amity, about thirty miles from here. I think I will wait till tomorrow to go visit him."

Rick got up early the next day so he could drive to Amity and catch the brother before he went to work. He drove by the station and picked up Randy who was waiting outside for him.

"With a name like Samson Smith, he ought to be easy to locate," thought Rick as he drove through the small town.

"I guess the first place to look would be the police station," continued Rick mumbling to himself.

"Rick Smears, detective," he said as he flipped his badge open.

"I'm looking for Samson Smith," replied Rick.

"Ok, let me look, wait I know him, he is the owner of a pawn shop a couple blocks from here," said the police officer on duty.

"Thanks," replied Rick as he headed to the door.

"Got an address," he told Randy as they drove down the streets, noticing that some were paved, some brick, and some were just dirt. After about five minutes of driving through town, they reached the pawn shop.

The bell rang on the door as Rick entered.

"Looking for anything in particular?" asked Samson.

"Well to tell you the truth, I'm trying to track down a particular necklace. We have had several murders and this necklace keeps turning up but it seems to also disappear," said Rick.

"Is it the one that was on my brother's neck?" asked Samson.

"Could be. You got it?" returned with a question.

"Let me look……no I remember, I sold it this morning," stated Samson.

"Do you know who?" asked Rick.

"Yes, he is a friend of mine, Kevin Michaels. Said he wanted to get it for his girlfriend".

"Got his address?" asked Rick.

"Sure, I'll write it down for you," replied Samson as he reached for a pen and a notepad.

"Thanks," replied Rick as Samson handed him the piece of paper.

Rick made a brief stop at a nearby café to grab a coffee to go, a quick respite during their busy day. As he and his partner sat in the car, meticulously reviewing the chain of events yet again, the distant wail of a siren cut through their conversation. Within moments, a police car raced past the café, its siren blaring, drawing their immediate attention.

Finishing the last sip of his coffee, Rick casually discarded the empty cup into the back seat. His demeanor quickly shifted as he started the car and accelerated to follow the speeding police vehicle. As they neared a residential street, Rick's eyes were drawn to a house with flashing red and blue lights illuminating the front yard. It matched the address Samson had provided earlier, confirming his suspicions. This was the location they had been seeking.

In the front yard, a woman was wielding a large kitchen knife, her movements erratic and threatening as she swung it aggressively at a man who appeared to be her boyfriend. The scene was chaotic, but Rick's trained eye quickly assessed the situation. He surmised that the man matched the description Samson had provided at the pawn shop earlier—a detail that now seemed crucial.

Rick's attention was drawn to the woman's neck, where a necklace dangled, catching the light with each of her volatile motions. It was unmistakable—the item they had been searching for. Acting on instinct, Rick called out to the nearby officer as he stepped out of the car with urgency.

"Remove the necklace!" Rick commanded, his voice firm despite the absurdity of the directive. He felt a fleeting moment of self-doubt at the simplicity of his plan, but under the circumstances, he knew there was little to lose.

The policeman shot Rick a look that combined both confusion and skepticism but decided to act regardless. As he cautiously reached for the necklace, the woman's erratic movement caused the knife to swing dangerously close to his forearm. Despite the near miss, he managed to snatch the necklace and toss it to the ground in one swift motion.

In an instant, the woman's demeanor changed completely. She dropped the knife and collapsed to her knees, her hands trembling. Tears streamed down her face as she stammered, "What is going on?" Her eyes fell to the blood staining her jeans, and panic began to set in. "What did I do?" she whispered, her voice breaking. Turning to her boyfriend, she noticed the shallow knife wound on his right arm and gasped. "I'm so sorry," she said, her voice filled with remorse.

Kevin exchanged a quick glance with the officer and gave a subtle wave, dismissing him.

"You sure?" the policeman asked, his tone laced with hesitation.

"Yes, I'm sure," Kevin replied firmly. "I'll grab some bandages and take care of it."

The officer, however, shook his head. "Sorry, but I can't just let it slide. I'm required to file a report. If he chooses not to press charges, that's up to him, but this incident has to be documented," Officer Leonard explained apologetically.

Meanwhile, Rick, maintaining his composure, retrieved the discarded necklace. Using a pencil to avoid contaminating evidence, he carefully held it up and examined the back. His eyes narrowed as he read the inscription etched into the metal, piecing together another part of the puzzle.

"Beware of the unseen force"

Rick scanned the area and spotted an empty glass jar. Moving quickly, he carefully placed the necklace inside, sealed the lid tightly, and held the jar up to examine it for any gaps.

"I'm not taking any chances," he muttered under his breath, cradling the jar protectively under his arm as he strode back to the car. A moment of doubt flickered across his face as he thought aloud, "Bury it somewhere safe, far away from anyone it could harm... What am I saying? It's just a necklace."

After dropping Randy off at his apartment, Rick went straight home, his mind racing with unease. The weight of the situation pressed on him, despite the absurdity of his plan.

Later that night, Rick stood in his backyard, the jar tucked securely under one arm. His property bordered the edge of the park's playground, a serene but public area. He waited until darkness blanketed the neighborhood, determined to avoid the curious gaze of any children or passersby. Under the dim light of the stars, he began digging, intent on ensuring the necklace—and whatever power it might hold—was hidden and forgotten.

Three months after the incident, Detective Rick decided it was time for a fresh start and moved across town. The whirlwind of cases he had tackled since then had pushed the memory of the jar he had buried in the backyard to the far recesses of his mind.

Not long after his departure, the property was purchased by a young couple, the Wilsons, who moved in with their energetic son, Sean. The family settled into the house, unaware of the secrets the backyard held.

Six months later, on a sunny afternoon, young Sean was exploring the yard when his small shovel struck something solid beneath the soil. Curious, he dug deeper and uncovered a glass jar. Inside was an old necklace, its appearance intriguing but unassuming to the boy.

Excited by his discovery, Sean ran to his mother, who was in the middle of hosting a garage sale on their driveway. She was engrossed in conversation with a customer and barely noticed as Sean placed the jar on one of the tables alongside the other items for sale. Growing impatient, Sean left the jar behind and darted across the street to join his friend Billie for an afternoon of play, blissfully unaware of the significance of what he had found.

"Do you go to garage sales? Beware of the glass jar on the table, great bargain, eh? You may get more than you pay for".

I'd give anything if….

In a small suburban town in Iowa, the full moon disappeared behind the large thunderheads that were floating out of the western sky. A light breeze was beginning to pick up strength and blow the surrounding trees, as scattered streaks of lightning danced from cloud to cloud.

In her living room, the breeze blew the white sheer curtain across the back of the couch where Susan Waters was reading a mystery novel. Even though she had on her burgundy silk robe, the summer breeze sent a chill down her back. Susan didn't know whether it was because of the book she was reading or the storm that was blowing up in the southwest. Reaching back over the couch, she lowered the window and pulled the curtain back into place.

She rubbed her arms to make the goosebumps subside. Picking up the book once again, she began to read some more. After a while, Susan dropped the book on her lap and glanced out the window. She watched the storm moving ever so slowly towards her house. The lightning was licking the sky like a large serpent's tongue. There was a faint scratching on the roof of the house. After a few startling seconds, Susan realized that the wind was making the branch of her elm tree rake across the shingles on the roof with every gust of wind.

"Boy, I wish I didn't have to be alone in this house all night by myself! I'd give anything if we could get rich and John didn't have to work third shift, or any shift," Susan said, turning back to her book. After staring aimlessly at the words, she sighed, "I give up." She placed a small piece of paper between the pages she was reading and closed the book. After standing up and stretching, Susan turned off the light and placed the book on the end table. The lightning illuminated the house enough for her to see the way to her bedroom. After setting the alarm on the old-fashioned clock radio, she removed her robe and pulled back the covers. Climbing into bed and finally being able to close her eyes, she hoped sleep would overcome her quickly.

The lightning was so bright and the thunder so loud that sleep *was* almost impossible. Finally, after pulling the pillows over her head she drifted off to sleep. During the night, the storm raged on. The rain started slowly at first and then came down in torrents. It woke her up enough that she got up to close all the windows before it really started coming down. The awnings were helping block the light rain.

The next morning, Susan awoke at the sound of the radio. The sun rays coming through the bedroom window put her in a terrific mood, so she hopped up, took a shower, and headed for the kitchen to fix her husband's breakfast. John worked the 11-7 shift at the local factory.

At seven thirty John pulled into the driveway with his old white pick-up. He parked the truck, tossed a brick behind the rear wheel, as a precaution, and headed up the sidewalk towards the house. Susan opened the door and met him with a good morning kiss. She could smell the freshness caused by the storm from the night before. It had stopped sometime during the early morning hours. The sidewalk was still damp, except where the sun had already started doing its job.

"Hi honey," said John, "You sure look cheerful this morning.

Did you dream about me last night?"

Susan smiled and replied: "No. Sorry I didn't. The storm was so bad, I couldn't fall right to sleep. I covered my head during the worst part and finally fell into a deep sleep. But I did manage to get all the windows closed in time."

John finished his breakfast, kissed his wife, showered, and climbed into bed. This was his usual routine. Susan went on with her daily chores. She knew John's routine was one that he seldom changed.

It was almost ten o'clock when the front doorbell rang. Answering the door, Susan found a tall dark-haired man, dressed in a three-piece charcoal gray suit. His full beard was neatly trimmed, and Susan felt herself overwhelmed by his appearance. She considered her husband handsome, but occasionally she would find a man just a little better looking. This was one of those occasions.

"Good morning, ma'am. May I have a word with you?"

Susan could not resist. "Sure, but we'll have to talk out here, my husband just went to sleep."

"Perhaps I should come back when he is awake."

"That's alright. What can I help you with?"

"I am introducing a lottery game in this state. We are picking approximately fifty people to help promote it and your name was one of them.

Susan was confused, "Is this one of those things where I buy a ticket and if you draw my number, I win?" The handsome visitor smiled broadly, "I believe you must have heard of the lottery already."

"Yes. I have. I've just never heard of anyone going door to door."

"As I have said, this is a special promotion offer. Now would you be interested in one of our tickets?"

"How much?" Susan was looking for her purse.

"Oh, there is no obligation...yet." the man answered.

"What do you mean, yet?" Susan was beginning to become confused, and maybe a little suspicious.

"A ...Well, you know such things as taxes and fees come later." said the stranger with a smile.

"Alright. How many tickets can I get?"

"This is just a promotion. Only a fifty people are allowed to receive them. The limit is one. I am truly sorry."

Susan wasn't surprised at his answer. Nothing is free anyway. "Oh, that's fine. I probably won't win anyway. I never do."

Pulling out a ticket, the stranger handed it to her, and wished her good luck. He told her he had a few more tickets to pass out quickly because the drawing was tonight at midnight and that she could check for her number in the morning newspaper. With that said, he turned to leave.

"Thanks!" yelled Susan, as she watched the man walk towards his car. He responded with a cursory wave of his hand as he got in the car and drove down the street.

Susan went back in the house and placed the ticket under a decorative magnet she had on the side of the refrigerator. Hesitating for a moment, she looked at the number and made a mental note to check the paper first thing in the morning to see if she had won.

Still daydreaming about what she would do if by chance she would win, Susan continued on with her housework.

It was nearly three in the afternoon before John stirred from the bedroom. After he had a cup of "go juice", Susan told him about the lottery ticket. Grunting at the news, John picked up the paper and began thumbing through the sports section. He knew his wife was always sending in all the sweepstakes entries hoping to get rich quick. That evening, they sat down to watch television before John had to go to work. He was in his boxer shorts and t-shirt. Not one word was said about the new lottery. Susan knew better. John would just start arguing about it.

After the sports telecast had finished, John dressed for work, kissed his wife and said goodbye to her. She handed him lunch she had packed for him, gave him a peck on the cheek and smiled while he got into his truck and drove off to work.

Susan curled up on the couch with the same book she had been reading the night before. After a couple of hours and chapters later, she placed the marker in the book and went to bed. There was no storm to keep her awake tonight, just a full moon looking in under the awning of the window.

When she woke, Susan got the paper as she did every morning and sat at the kitchen table. She was still in her pajamas and had made coffee, before she sat down. Susan got up from the table and went over to the counter to pour herself a cup. She had time to read the paper before she would fix her husband's breakfast. Turning to the page which had the numbers of the daily lottery and reading the line of four digits.

"It can't be!" gasped Susan as she looked towards the fridge and the lottery ticket hanging there. She sat there for a few seconds longer, afraid to look at the ticket itself. The excitement was building inside her. Finally jumping up, she hurried over and jerked the ticket out from under the magnet,

"The numbers match! I won!" she yelled at no one. As she was jumping up and down and spinning around holding the ticket to her chest.

John's truck came up the driveway. Susan went running out to meet him. She threw her arms around her husband's neck and told him the good news.

"Are you sure? Did you double check the number carefully?"

"Look for yourself," she said, handing him the paper and ticket. Susan could hardly contain herself as the pair walked from the driveway to the house. John told her to wait a minute, he had to grab his lunch bucket and shut the door of the truck.

Once inside, John took the paper and matched the numbers on the ticket himself. Sure enough, they matched. He gave his wife a big hug and apologized for griping about her entering all those contests. Then he picked her up in his arms, hugged her and swirled around the kitchen a couple of times. As he put her down, the front doorbell rang.

John and Susan were both surprised by the doorbell this early in the morning. Susan went to the front door and opened it to the very same man who had stood there the day before talking about lottery tickets.

"Congratulations!" he said to her, extending his hand.

Susan passed up the hand and gave the man a big hug, then stopped, short. "But how did you know so soon?"

"I keep records on the people I pass the tickets out to. I also get up at 4:00 am to start my trip around. The numbers were drawn at midnight. "Now, if you'll sign this paper, I'll leave you with the check for your winnings and then I'll be on my way."

"What? Is that all? Just sign a paper? Don't we have to go down to the lottery office?" asked Susan.

"It just shows that I've given you the money," replied the stranger holding out a pen and the clipboard with an official looking paper fastened to it.

"I thought we had to go to the state capital and claim the money," John spoke up.

"Not in this case," replied the stranger.

Susan was so excited that she didn't read the fine print. Once she finished, the man handed her the check for one million dollars and left.

John quit his job the following week. The next few months were full of excitement for the young couple. They went on tours and cruises and bought everything they had ever wanted or longed for. Everything was going fine. Then six months to the day after Susan had received the check, she received a red envelope in the mail. It was addressed to her. Inside was an invitation to Chicago for her to a party for all the winners.

#2

The small, one room apartment contained a bed, sink, refrigerator, and a small gas range. The paint was peeling off the walls and the floor was covered with all the various scraps of mismatched tile that the landlord could find. There was only one window. A shade ripped halfway through the middle. The window faced the rear of a large warehouse. A trash littered alley ran between the buildings. Rats could be seen forging amidst the boxes and broken bottles.

In the center of this poverty-stricken room was a table and two wobbly chairs. Sitting on one of those chairs was a young man named Jim Thompson. With his head resting on his arms. Jim was thinking about his situation. He had been out of work for several weeks. The only steel plant in Pine Ridge, where he had been employed for five years, had closed their doors permanently.

"I'd give anything, if I could get out of this dump. Just find some place where there was work. I've looked everywhere..." he said out loud, but talking to himself.

He was interrupted by a rapping on his door.

"Go away, I'm busy and I don't have any money!" snapped Jim as he raised his head from his arms, then lowered it back down again.

The visitor was persistent with his knocking.

"You heard me! Go away!" he yelled as he raised his head up once more. Still the knocking continued. Jim couldn't take it any longer.

"Alright, alright. I'm coming. When I get there and open the door, it better be important!" Jim stood up forcefully and the chair fell over on the floor, making him more irritated.

He opened the door and found a stranger standing there with a sheepish grin on his face.

"Jim Thompson?" he asked, extending his hand in friendship.

"Look, Mac, I told you. I don't have any money, so I can't buy anything you're offering!"

The man just smiled at Jim; his hand still extended in a friendly gesture.

"Excuse me. I'm not selling. I'm giving. Giving away tickets. That is...it's a promotional project."

"Tickets? To where?" asked Jim.

"Not to where, to what." The gentleman answered.

"All right, smart ass, to what?"

"To win a million dollars! answered the stranger.

"Oh sure. And I'm George Washington, too" Jim had had about enough of this visitor.

"I can leave, but I'm sure you won't want me to after I tell you your ticket will be free."

"Free?" Jim paused, "Ok, I'll bite. Tell me more."

"This is a promotional project for a lottery. We are giving away fifty tickets at a time, hoping to draw in more people. It's a daily drawing."

"Alright, I'll take one. I'll never win though. I never have had good luck with the lottery."

The stranger handed Jim the ticket and explained that this special drawing was tonight at midnight and the results would be in the morning paper. He then bid him farewell and left Jim to ponder the whole situation. The next morning, Jim walked down to the corner newsstand and thumbed through the morning paper. He was looking through the work ads. Turning to the last page, he found the numbers that were drawn for that day. Sure enough, there were the four numbers and they matched Jim's ticket.

"Hey! If you are not buying it, beat it!" yelled the newsstand owner.

"I won!" yelled Jim at the top of his voice.

Dropping the paper on the ground, Jim ran back to his apartment. The newsstand owner picked up the crumbled paper and scratched his head "What in the world is wrong with him?"

Jim burst into his apartment and started looking around. There was nothing in there that he couldn't do without. Besides, he could buy everything new.

A knock-sound sounded from the door.
"Come in!" yelled Jim. "Who could that be?" he thought. Nobody ever comes to see him at his crappy apartment.

As the door opened, Jim recognized the man who had given him the ticket the day before. "Hi guy. Come on in. I won! Did you see it? I actually won!"

"Yes, I know. I have the check with me. All I need is your signature showing that I gave it to you."

"Sure, hand it here," replied Jim anxiously.

Jim signed the form without hesitation. He handed the signed document back. The stranger gave him the check and after shaking hands with Jim, left.

The next few months, Jim spent wildly. His first purchase was a better place to live, a new condo. Then he bought new clothes, a new gold colored Pontiac Firebird like he had always dreamed about.

Six months from the day that Jim received the check, he received a red envelope in the mail. An invitation along with a ticket on an airline to Chicago.

#3

The shot rang out, echoing through the alley in Townsville, Kentucky. A young kid, about fourteen years old, dropped to the dirty pavement. A brown paper sack tumbled down the street past the officer who held the fatal weapon.

Officer Tom Morris yelled "Stop!" *As* he did, the kid had turned on his heels and shot at him. The bullet grazed Tom's left arm.

Immediately Tom had fired upon the assailant. The bullet found its mark and the kid dropped. He walked up to the kid with his gun still drawn. When he was within ten feet, the officer stopped and moved cautiously towards the form still grasping the gun in his right hand. Slowly, Tom reached down and felt the young man's pulse. No pulse, he was dead. The bullet had found its mark. "Crap, I've killed him," said Tom as he lowered his own pistol to his holster.

"It was self-defense," replied his partner, Paul Simmons, as he walked up behind Tom. "I saw the whole thing. He fired first."

"That isn't the point, Paul. He's only a kid!" Tom stared at the lifeless body. "What is this world coming to? Kids with guns, shooting at people, getting killed themselves"

Paul didn't reply. He reached out and put his hand on Tom's shoulder.

Turning to look at Paul, Tom remarked, "You know, I'd give anything to get a different job. I'm tired of chasing crooks and finding them to be no older than fourteen or fifteen."

They waited for the ambulance to pick up the body. Then they returned to the station to make out their reports, leaving the crime crew to do their thing with the whole situation.

Paul left the station first and went home. He had told the chief his story and told Tom goodnight. He knew that tomorrow would be one frantic day for Tom, with the inquest and having to tell how and why he pulled the trigger.

Tom went for a cold beer and another night of haunting dreams.

The next day Tom went to a hearing to prove his innocence. It was classified self-defense and Tom was returned to duty. After the hearing the boy's parents cursed him as he left the courtroom. Tom was feeling low. This had happened before and he knew it probably wouldn't be the last.

As he left the courthouse, he met a man standing on the steps. He was dressed in a three-piece suit and sported a neatly trimmed beard.

"Thomas Morris?" asked the man approaching him.

"Yes?" questioned Tom.

"I would like to take a minute of your time and introduce you to a lottery," said the stranger.

"Look Mac, I've got too much on my mind to mess with any lottery right now!" replied Tom.

"There is no obligation, yet." replied the man.

"What do you mean, yet?" asked Tom.

"You know, oh...taxes and things like that."

"Oh", mumbled Tom. He started walking down the steps towards the sidewalk, The stranger reached out and touched Tom's shoulder. The light touch stopped Tom in his tracks.

"Look, I don't like pushy people. If you don't leave me alone, I'll arrest you!" replied Tom as he walked to his car and got in the driver's seat.

The stranger kept up with him. He walked up to the passenger's side and tossed the ticket in the open window into the front seat. "The drawing is at midnight tonight. Just check your paper.

Tom hit the steering wheel with the palms of his hands.

"Damn it! I've had enough of you, you jerk!" said Tom as he got out of the car.

Looking towards the other side of the car where the man had just been, he found nothing. Looking up and down the street, there was no sign of the stranger. However, he did notice a black car, speeding up the street. "Must have been in one heck of a hurry," said Tom as he looked at the tail lights.

"I wonder how he knew my name?" he thought as he got back in the car. He picked up the ticket, glanced absently at it. Then stuck it in his pocket, and headed home.

Tom had another sleepless night interrupted by the "the same nightmare," as before. The nightmare of the kid dropping to the ground. Looking at the clock once again, which felt like the hundredth time that night; it was a few minutes after five. He made up his mind, he was going to call in today. Besides, his boss told him to take a couple days off.

Staying up, he waited for the morning paper to arrive. Sitting there at the table he held his head in his hands, trying to get rid of the sight of that kid's lifeless body hitting the pavement. He was brought back to reality as the paper hit the storm door. He jumped and almost knocked his third cup of coffee on the floor. "Come on, Tom, pull it together!" he said aloud as he got up pushing the chair back. He headed for the door to get the paper.

After retrieving it, he sat back down at the table, with another cup of coffee. He opened the paper to the points of interest to him. He was about to toss the paper in the trash when he noticed the lottery numbers on the back page. The numbers seemed to jump out at him, attracting his attention.

"Now, what did I do with that ticket?" Tom said to himself.

Tom reached up and rubbed his chin, making a coarse sound from him not having shaved yet.

"Ah, I remember now! I put it in my jacket pocket." Tom exclaimed as he headed to the closet.

After he pulled the ticket out of his jacket pocket, he matched up the numbers. Tom slumped back in the kitchen chair. Holding the ticket at arm's length, he couldn't believe it.

"I won!" he yelled at no one, not caring who heard him. He was rich.

"Never again will I have to pull the trigger on some young kid," he continued. "I can quit and find a different place to live, far away from here".

Finishing his coffee, Tom decided he needed to dress in more than just his boxer shorts, so he went to his closet and grabbed a shirt and some blue jeans, figuring he would have to drive to the state capital to cash his ticket. He went out to the garage, and started to get in his car. Since he had already called in to the station to take some time off, he might as well go collect his money. As he opened the car door and had one leg inside; he was stopped by a tap on the passenger side window. It was the same man that gave him the ticket yesterday. The garage door was open to let Tom leave.

"Where are you going, Tom?" he asked with a smile.

"I'm going to the capital to cash my ticket. I won!" replied Tom.

"Yes, that's what I figured you would do... that is why I am here. I keep records of these things. There is no need for you to go anywhere. I have the check with me. You see, since this is a promotional give away for this lottery, we have to make sure the winners receive their winnings personally."

Tom stood there with a questionable look.

"New Lottery," was all the stranger would say.

"I've also never heard of it being done this way," added Tom.

"Excuse me. If you will quit talking, I'll give you the check for one million dollars and be on my way."

"All of it now? I thought we only got part of it annually?' asked Tom."

"Promotional," was the only thing the stranger would say. He handed the clipboard to Tom. Tom signed it in a hurry. He was like a little child waiting to get a piece of candy. Handing Tom a crisp white check with dark red lettering, the stranger bid Tom farewell.

"Hey I didn't catch your name?" asked Tom, as the stranger walked away. The stranger didn't answer, he just tossed his arm towards the sky in a quick wave and left.

Tom stood there staring at his check. He had never seen so many zeroes on a check in his life, especially on a check made out in his name.

During the next few months, Tom spent a lot of his money on things he always wanted but couldn't afford. He bought a new house in a town about seventy miles away. He took vacations, threw parties, and really enjoyed his new wealth.

Six months went by and Tom received a red envelope. Upon opening the red envelope, he found an invitation to a party being held near Chicago the following week. Included an airline ticket. The party was a reunion of the millionaire winners.

"Well, why not? Might be interesting to meet some of the other winners," said Tom as he walked over to the calendar and wrote the date down so he wouldn't miss it.

#4

Jimmy Williams was a Hoosier. He lived in Indiana all his life. He was now seventeen. He had been an amputee since he was seven years old. He and his father had gone to a ball game. After the ball game they headed home and were involved in a horrible accident. His father had been killed and he lost his leg. Jimmy was limited on his childhood activities. He really missed his father greatly. He was confined to a wheelchair. His mom apologized, telling him she just couldn't afford an artificial leg. The people in the other vehicle didn't have insurance.

He used to sit in his wheelchair in the park for hours watching the other children playing baseball and football.

One afternoon while watching a game, Jimmy looked over at his mom and asked, "Why can't I have an artificial leg? Why do I have to sit here and be stared at like I'm some kind of animal in a zoo? Why mom? Why?" asked Jimmy through tearful eyes.

Jimmy's mother looked at her son with great regret in her voice as she replied. "Your father's insurance didn't leave us much after the funeral and I can't afford it myself. Ever since your father was killed in that wreck, it has been hard to make ends meet. The hospital bill is still so large...."

"But mom, I'd give anything to have enough money so you wouldn't have to worry anymore. And I could have a leg."

"I know Jimmy, but don't be that way. I know you mean well, but we could be a lot worse off.

"I don't care anymore. I'd give anything to be able to run like the rest of the kids do."

Jimmy's mother ignored him and went back to watching the football game. She felt sorry for her son sitting there bound to that steel chair.

The sun was starting to get low in the western sky. Louise took hold of the handles on the wheelchair and gave it a slight push to get it in motion. "It's time we left, Jimmy."

"I know mom, sorry for what I said earlier"

Just as Jimmy's mother turned the wheelchair towards the apartment building, which was behind the park. A hand touched her on the shoulder. Louise jumped and made the wheelchair jerk.

"Sorry, didn't mean to startle you," said the man standing behind her.

He was dressed in a three-piece charcoal suit.

"Ma'am, are you Louise Williams? Mother of Jimmy?" asked the stranger.

"Yes, I am. Whom may I ask, is inquiring?"

My name is not important. I'm promoting a lottery and your son has been chosen to receive a free ticket.

Since he is a minor, you will be allowed to receive it for him."

"I don't know...."

"Go ahead mom. He said it was free!" interrupted Jimmy.

"Well, I guess, " answered Louise. "Are you sure it's free?"

"Yes, please take it. Jimmy may win, you never know. Check your paper tomorrow as the drawing is at midnight tonight."

Louise extended her hand and the stranger placed the ticket in her palm. He bid them farewell and headed for his car. Louise and her son continued on towards their building discussing the possibilities if they won.

After they had supper and watched a couple shows on television, Jimmy said he wanted to go to bed.

As his mother was helping him get into bed, he looked at her and said, "I love you mom. Don't forget to check the paper in the morning."

"I love you too, son. Now you get some sleep," she said as she leaned over to kiss Jimmy good night.

Louise didn't think much of the idea of a lottery ticket. She had never won anything in her life before and she figured it was a waste of time now.

The next morning started with a scream from Louise, which woke Jimmy immediately. "Mom, what's wrong? Are you alright?"

Jimmy had always been afraid something would happen to her and he wouldn't be able to help her because of his leg.

"Son! Son! Jimmy honey! I've won! *I* won! Let me rephrase that, we won!" shouted Louise with great enthusiasm as she rushed into his room.

"Won? Won what? You mean the ticket was a winner'?"

"Sure was! Now we can pay the hospital bill off, buy our own place, and the most important thing of all, we can get you that leg!"

Jimmy gave his mother a big hug. They both sat on his bed for a few minutes staring at the ticket's numbers and the numbers in the paper. Then she helped Jimmy get dressed. Both of them skipped breakfast. They were too excited to eat.

Jimmy and his mother were deciding how they would go about getting to the state capital, to claim their money, when they heard a knock at the door.

"Congratulations!" said the man who had given them the ticket.

"Yeah! Thanks a lot!" Jimmy spoke up, extending his hand.

"Now if you'll be so kind as to sign here, Jimmy, on this line and have your mother sign the bottom of the page, I'll give you the check.'"

"You mean we don't have to go to the state capital?"

"Oh no! Now you, Louise," said the man handing the paper to her after Jimmy had finished signing.

"What is that?" she asked, nodding at the paper she had just signed.

"It's just a statement; it shows that you have received the money from me."

"All right," replied Louise as she signed the paper and gave it back to the man. He then handed them the chock.

After putting the money in the bank, Louis made Jimmy an appointment to be fitted for the new leg next week.

They went anywhere they wanted, bought anything they desired and paid off all their bills. They bought a new house and went shopping for furniture.

After Jimmy had received his artificial leg and had gotten used to using it. They went on long trips to see the countryside. The money they had won changed their lives.

Six months had passed since the day Louise and Jimmy received the ticket. She walked out to her mailbox to get the morning mail and found only one letter. It was a red envelope addressed to Jimmy. Returning to the house with the intriguing envelope, she gave it to her son.

"Far out, mom! It's an invitation to a party for all the million-dollar lottery winners. There is also a ticket in here for the airlines!"

Louise felt good inside. It was the first invitation her son had ever received to go to a party. He was almost eighteen.

He was doing very well with his new leg and she decided to let him go.

"Are you going, mom?" asked Jimmy.

"The invitation is for you, son. You are eighteen now. You are an adult. You don't need me to babysit you. Please go and have fun. Besides, I got plenty I can do. I may even go shopping by myself. That man also told me there was going to be fifty winners altogether. Maybe you'll meet some new people and make some new friends."

THE GATHERING

The estate where the party was to be held looked as if it had been transported out of some spooky movie. A large iron gate guarded the entrance to the drive. The gates were hinged from a stone wall that surrounded the entire estate. Vines of ivy had overtaken the walls. The gates themselves opened inward towards a huge yard overgrown with vegetation. Several weeping willow trees were almost hidden behind the rows of evergreen trees. A badly cracked cement walk wound its way through the dense trees. Clumps of grass stuck up through the breaks in the walkway. In other words, the estate had not been kept up by the property owners. This only enhanced the eerie spooky view.

At the far end of the walk was an expansive structure silhouetted in the moonlight. There were large towers on each side of the main part of the house. Several small windows were located all around the towers, but very few were visible on the side section. The ones that could be seen were located at the front.

Two grotesque statues perched on a large ledge above the massive doors. Red lights gleamed from their eyes, casting an eerie glow around the entrance.
It was the sixth of June. The guests would soon arrive. At five o'clock, the first cab pulled up in front of the iron gates. Within the hour all of the guests had arrived.

There were fifty in all, gathered inside the large main room. A fireplace was located directly across from the entrance and the whole wall was covered in brick. The other three walls were painted in a deep wine color. Every ten feet a torch was placed in a holder that was attached to the wall. There was no evidence of electricity in the room. The floor was covered in a deep maroon carpet. The furniture consisted of two couches and two easy chairs, with several folding chairs aligning the walls.

"I wonder where or who our ..." one of the guests started to ask, but was interrupted by a deep voice in the shadows. "Good evening, my guests. I am your host. It was my party that you were invited to, I'm overwhelmed to see that you all made it to... shall we say the "Gathering"? A hideous laugh escaped the lips of the stranger as he threw his head back. He had overheard Susan remark that it was too warm in the room.

"I'm sorry Susan. It will get much hotter before the night is through."

The guests looked at each other in bewilderment. They mumbled amongst themselves, asking where the food and drinks wore that went with any party.

This is my entertainment," said the host, holding up fifty pieces of paper.

"What is that?" asked Tom.

"These? These are the papers that you foolishly signed to receive your million dollars! Each one of you!"

"Who are you?" yelled Tom.

There was no answer, just that same laugh once more. "I'm leaving this place," yelled Jimmy.

With that remark, the host raised his arms and the door faded away. The guests started screaming and yelling to be let out. The host raised his hand again and the guests stopped the screaming to hear what he was going to say now.

Once the noise subsided, the host spoke once again. "Each of you said you would do anything or give anything if.... Well, you didn't read the fine print when you signed the paper. You signed your souls over to me." Those were the last words. He raised his arms and the walls were engulfed in flames.

They were falling over each other, yelling, shoving, and screaming trying to find a way out of this hell. It was useless, they had signed their souls over to the Prince of Darkness because they had said, "I'd give anything if...."

Days later the police came in search of the missing people. There was no trace of the address they had been given no evidence that any type of building had ever been on the lot where the address had directed them.

"I don't understand it," replied one officer. "Fifty people don't just disappear. I was informed by a cab driver that he took a fare to this address. He said he let them out but there was no house there that he could see. There hasn't been a house here for many years. It just doesn't make sense. The only thing that is here is an old broken-down iron gate and an open field surrounded by a stone wall. What do we do now chief?"

"You got me George. I'd give anything to find out what happened to those fifty people...."

The End??

Be careful what you wish for, you may get it and more....

What's For Dinner?

Nathen Hanns was a man of conflicting interests. Besides being the owner of a large grocery store, Nathen was the owner of a mortuary. Over the years he had become a shrewd businessman and would cut corners whenever possible in order to save a dollar.

On one particular evening, Nathen sat at his early American desk figuring out his budget.
The books for both businesses were showing a lower income than what he had become accustomed to. Nathen slammed the books closed on the desk and went into the kitchen to make himself another cup of coffee. His kitchen was modest. No new appliances or any decorations. Although Hanns had wealth; he kept it all in the bank. He was much more like Ebenezer Scrooge. He didn't like to spend any money if he could keep from it. He was obsessed with the balance of his accounts.

"If there was only a way to make both businesses more profitable," thought Nathen as he leaned against the counter sipping at his cup.

Everything had seemed to go downhill since the drought that had started in the summer a few years ago and had continued. The pastures had dried up, forcing a lot of farmers to either feed their cattle the hay they had stocked up or take them to market. More than a few of the beasts didn't make it and died from starvation. This caused the prices of beef to rise sharply. The price of hamburger soared.

Nathen finished his coffee and retired to the meager living room for the evening. While he appeared to watch the evening news, his mind was still going over the numbers he had seen earlier.

The next morning, he went to his grocery store to get things going. On the way there, he turned on the radio. He wanted to be informed of the price of beef. While he waited for the news, he listened to the DJ with his morning chatter. When the news did finally come back on, he found that the price of most meats had just risen again earlier that morning. Hearing this bit of news made his spirits drop even lower. He knew he would have to raise the prices of hamburger again to keep up with the market. He also knew that a lot of people would be passing right on by the meat freezer when they saw the new higher prices.

This was too much. Nathan was now too upset to go to the store and headed for his mortuary. On the way there, he turned his attention back to the car radio only to hear that a mortuary in the next town had installed a cremation furnace. They were now offering lower prices for cremation services than services using caskets.

"Damn! I can't win for losing!" said Nathen as he hit the steering wheel with the palm of his hand.

Arriving at the mortuary, he drove to the rear entrance where he found his employee with a body that was just being brought in.

"What happened to this one Eric?" asked Nathen.

Eric was Nathen's helper. He transported the bodies to the funeral home after the coroner had completed his part of the process.

"I believe he was involved in a wreck of some sort," replied Eric.

Nathen Hanns unzipped the black body bag and looked at the body. The lower part of the body looked like it had been through a meat grinder.

"At least we are still getting business. The family could have gone to that new crematory" replied Eric with a chuckle.

"I'm just glad the top half isn't damaged too much. Remarked Hanns. "It will make it so much simpler for us. Since we only have to open the top half of the casket. I don't like closed casket funerals."

"Well, do the best you can. Hanns continued. You always do such a good job in these circumstances. I think I'll head back home and take it easy the rest of the day. Got this headache I can't seem to get rid of."

Nathen returned home, but not to take it easy. He sat at his desk the rest of the day, except for getting a cup of coffee. Knowing he could trust Eric to get the necessary things done before the final preparations, which Nathen would perform later.

Nathen was trying to figure out what he could do so that he could somehow come out ahead. The next morning, Nathen was reading the paper and noticed that the price of hamburger had jumped another quarter a pound. All beef had jumped, but Nathen was more interested in the hamburger price.

Nathen knew that when the price went up, he would have to order less. He just couldn't afford to have any of the meat in inventory to spoil before it was sold.

"When is all this going to end? Hamburgers are becoming like the precious stones that no one can afford."

As he sat there looking at the grocery store ads, he tried to figure out what he could do to make some kind of profit from the hamburger. He knew the ads might help some but he needed something more.

After sitting there for more than an hour and coming up blank. He continued to read the rest of the paper.

The accident of the man Eric had brought to the mortuary yesterday was on the last page. Apparently, the man had been hit by a train and his lower half had been crushed by the motor of his car.

The sight of those crushed legs kept flashing through his mind, along with the price of hamburger. Both businesses mingled in his mind. The high costs, the mangled legs, the store closing, the mortuary closing. Over and over these things kept rolling around in his head.

That's it!" said Nathen. "I got it. I'm going to order that new meat grinder for the store!"

Two weeks later, John Cooper was grilling hamburgers for his family on the grill.

"Honey, these hamburgers have a weird smell", he commented as he turned one of the burgers over on the rack.

"Aw, it's just probably the filler they put in them.

"Maybe that's it", mumbled John.

John didn't say anything else until he took a bite into one of the hamburgers. Then he reached two fingers to his lips and pulled out a small object.

"My God Beth! It's a toenail!"

The Fountain

The cafe and gas station set off the highway about 100 feet. The buildings were starting to show wear and tear from the weather. Age of the buildings was hard to determine, since they had survived several decades. Bob Wilson wasn't too happy, but his father had told him that someday this great paradise would be his. There were a couple rooms out back which was their livings quarters. Small but two small bedrooms and an attached patio. One bathroom had been installed next to bedrooms. It certainly wasn't a castle but it was home to him and his parents. Tom and Bob together had built a small shed which they called the maintenance room.

Bob did some research and found that one of his grandfathers had started this place as a watering hole for people traveling down the trail from one town to another. It was kind of a rest area. The old well still stood where it had originally been. The water that was used, still came from that same well. It was pumped to both of the buildings which made the little rest stop, a little more modern. After learning this information, Bob had changed his feelings about inheriting the place. He thought he would give it a try.

He stood in front of the two buildings, looking at the surroundings. The gas station and cafe stood alone against the backdrop of timber... It was surrounded by the woods on all sides except for the highway cutting through. There were several miles down the road in each direction to the next town.

If you looked closely at the buildings and studied the construction, you could see the years of renovation. From a little shack, to a gas station with two pumps and a cafe about forty feet long. Nothing was big or fancy, it was just a short rest and refresh from the long drive through the countryside.

Bob had a favorite spot in the timber where he would go to enjoy the view of nature. Birds and an occasional deer. It was just a small trail he had found. He felt like he was getting away from everything. The quiet, the animals and the timber just seemed to be in a different world.

One afternoon, he went to his "get away" place. It was on a small hill looking down towards the buildings. He sat there looking at the rest area. It reminded him of a giant bow holding together a cement ribbon, which wrapped the trees in a giant package.

Bob sat there recalling the day his dad told him he was going to sign the place over to him. He would get it all, since he was the only child and his mom agreed. Bob would take over the small business when the time came for them to retire. It didn't bring a lot of income but just enough to survive. His dad suggested he find a part time job in the next town.

Tom Wilson was Bob's father. Tom worked for a local oil company. He was what they called a "trouble shooter". He figured out their problem and told them how to fix it. Tom had to travel a lot and Bob and his mother ran the little rest stop. During one of Tom's trips, he stopped in a small town called Rossville, Arkansas and had dinner at the restaurant there...While sitting there at the table he decided to check out the peaceful community. Tom was always intrigued by small towns. He knew what it was like to have a small business and the low income it provided.

He spotted a store with the words, "Odd and Oddities" on the window that attracted his attention. After eating his lunch, which he thought was exceptional food, he walked down the street to the shop. As he entered the door, he looked over all the merchandise for a few minutes. Not finding anything of interest, he started to leave. A voice from the back of the store asked if he could help him. The owner didn't want to take a chance of losing a sale.

"Hi, my name is Mark," he said, extending his hand in a friendly manner. Need some help?"

"Nah, just killing time. Thought I'd check out what you had," answered Tom.

"Are you married? I'm not prying, I thought maybe you could take something home to the Mrs. You know, got to keep them happy," Mark said with a chuckle.

"True. Her and my son run our small cafe and gas station. Got any suggestions?"

Mark thought for a minute and rubbed his chin. "I might. Follow me." Leading Tom to the back of the store and then down the spiral staircase, he began to tell him about these items.

The Gift

"These items are very special. I don't tell all of my customers about them," said Mark as they reached the bottom step. Continuing on he said, "If people can't seem to find anything they want but I sense they would like to find something special I bring them down here."

Tom thought to himself, "what kind of bullshit is this?" He was about ready to turn around and go back up the steps. "This guy acts like one of those, carnival salesman. They keep pushing you to take more chances." Continued his thoughts.

"What's your wife and kids name?" trying to get Tom to relax

"Cathy and Bob," answered Tom.

"Where is your place located?" inquired Mark.

"It's out along the forest highway, as I call it. Not a whole lot of business, but we enjoy it. Well, they do. I enjoy it when I'm able to be there," said Tom.

"You may think that I'm full of it, but these items seem to fit the people I show them to," said Mark as he pointed to one fountain that was table top height. It was about 12 inches, from base to the very top. It looked like a large piece of wood with green leaves all around it.

"Wow, that is really cool!" said Tom. "I think I will take it. Cathy loves fountains."

"You sure have a lot of oddball items down here," observed Tom.

"Yep, sure do and each one has their own unique power, curse, or whatever you want to call it," answered Mark.

"Wow, I bet this place gets rather crazy at times," said Tom with a question in his voice.

"You don't know the half of it. I sold a man a big screen TV awhile back. A week later, I got police detectives knocking on my door. Apparently, the man turned up missing," said Mark as he continued up the steps. "I guess they thought he would be here," Mark said with a smile.

"If you see anything else, let me know," added Mark as he turned his head to talk over his shoulder.

Tom decided that the fountain was all he wanted for now. He did tell Mark he may come back some day and shop some more when he had more time.

The Unwrapping

Tom finished his work for the day and headed home. Once he parked the pick-up, he grabbed the box containing the fountain and called out for Bob.

"What's the problem? You sounded like you were hurt," asked Bob

"Sorry. No, I'm fine, but I had something I wanted to show you," replied Tom as he reached in the box, pulled out the fountain, and unwrapped the paper. Tom dropped the paper on the ground and extended his arm out to Bob, holding his treasure.

"What do you think of this? asked Tom.

Tom smiled but added, "Take a close look at it. It's a mix of grey and dark grey. There are no wires or batteries."

"Why did you buy that? If there is no power, or even a pump, how does it pump water? If it even does that?" asked Bob.

"I looked at it when I was in the truck. A small piece of parchment fell out of the bottom," said Tom as he was getting ready to take it inside.

"What did it say?" asked Bob

"It was really weird. It read" said Tom as he pulled the paper out.

> Water from a brook or stream
> That has had no human use for seen
> Fill the saucer to the top
> No more-no less-it will not stop
> Drink the water from the fount
> One day plus six is the count
> A thimble full is all you need
> To keep up your youth indeed
> Only one can use this gift
> Only one your age can lift
> So be careful which one you choose
> The other one you'll surely lose
> If you choose the gift to end
> Your current age would then begin
> One last warning you must hear
> Your youth draws strength from things so near

"After reading that, I think you ought to be the one to try it," said Tom, looking at Bob.

"Why me? You are the old man," said Bob with a smile.

"Well, I was thinking about the line, "Only one can use this gift". You are still young and have no wife. Hell, I don't even know if you have a girlfriend"

"We broke up a week ago. She didn't want to live out here. She wanted city life," said Bob.

"Oh well, someday you will find the right one," replied dad with a hug to Bob's shoulders.

"We read the paper and instructions. Let's take a good look at the fountain, said Tom as he set the table top fountain on one of the tables in the cafe.

"It looks like a piece of wood, with some green leaves stuck on the sides and a small tray around the bottom for water. So, what's so special about this? I could probably get one off the internet," added Bob. "Want me to get some water?"

"No. It said the water has to come from a brook or a stream," said Tom.

"Where are you going to get water from a stream out here in the woods?" asked Bob, with a smile.

"I was thinking, maybe you could take the truck to Heatherton and get a jug of water out of the creek that runs through the middle of town," replied Tom with a smile.

"What? Are you losing it? You believe in that crap?" asked Bob.

"Humor me son. You got anything better to do? It's only a forty-five-minute drive over there. I'll watch over the station. Your mom has the cafe," added Tom.

"Ok. I will grab one of those old milk jugs. Will that be enough?" asked Bob

"Oh yes. I think all we need is enough to fill the fountain."

"Besides, the guy that sold this fountain to me said he had several items in his store that had special powers or they are possessed, or something like that," added Tom.

"You got to be kidding me! And you believed him?" asked Bob.

Tom just shrugged his shoulders and looked up at his wife. She had been in the back of the cafe cleaning the floor and counters. As she was drying her hands on her apron she approached Tom's table.

"What cha got there?" she asked, looking at the fountain.

Tom began to explain everything to her and why he sent his son to Heatherton.

Cathy looked him in the eye and said, "You are going crazy. I agree with Bob."

Tom had put the fountain on a table in the back room. Hearing Bob return, he headed to retrieve the fountain. Bob walked in with the jug of fresh stream water, just as Tom came out of the back room with the fountain. They both set their items on the table and looked at each other.

"Are you going to put the water in it? I did go get it." asked Bob.

"No, I would rather you put the water in it," answered Tom.

"Good grief dad, don't you think you are carrying this a little too far?" asked Bob as he reached for the gallon jug.

"I am just curious, ok? By the way, place your other hand on the fountain as you fill it," added Tom.

Bob was tired of this fountain already, but he did as his dad requested. He placed his left hand on the top of the fountain and started pouring the water with his right. Immediately as the tray around the bottom started to fill, he felt a tingling sensation go through his body. He dropped the jug and jumped back, pulling his hand away at the same time.

"What the hell?" he asked, looking at his father.

"What's the matter?"

"It shocked me!" said Bob.

"You ok, son?" Asked Tom as he jumped up.

"Yeah, yeah, I'm ok. It was more of a tingling than a shock. Let's finish putting the water up to the edge and see what happens."

Bob finished pouring the tray full. Then setting the jug down, he placed his hands on the top and then moved them down to the sides   There was a little more tingling as Bob held on. Then the leaves started unfolding and getting greener. Little tiny holes opened up above each green leaf and water started oozing out. It ran across them and dropped down into the tray below.

"How is that possible?" asked Cathy.

"Beats me," replied Tom.

"Must be that strange power that that guy was talking about.

"How do you stop it?" asked Cathy, looking at it closely.

Tom and Bob looked at each other confused.

"Maybe you just dump the water off of it," stated Cathy heading back towards the kitchen.

"That ought to work," said Tom as he reached for the fountain. Streaks of electricity jumped from the fountain to Tom's hands.

"Shit, that doesn't work. You try it Bob," said Tom.

"Are you crazy? That's begging to get shocked," replied Bob.

"And who was saying it couldn't do anything because it doesn't have any power?"

"Ok, but I think it bonded with you," said Tom with a smile and a little chuckle.

"Let's not empty it just yet. Let it run for a few days and see if the water evaporates and it shuts itself off," suggested Bob.

"Ok, but we need to move it from here. I don't want someone to get shocked by it," said Tom as looked around the room searching for a way to move it.

"Alright, let me try touching it again. Remember, the second time I touched it all I got was a small tingle," said Bob.

He put a hand on each side and there was no tingling, just the cool water running down his arm. He lifted the fountain off the table and headed for the back room which they called the maintenance room. Setting it down on the bench, Bob stood there watching the water dripping off the leaves.

First Evidence

Two weeks had gone by and Bob was about ready to dump the water out of the fountain when he remembered about the thimble of water that was supposed to be consumed.

Tom was off on another troubleshooting trip. His mom was busy feeding a couple people that had stopped by for dinner.

Bob remembered the line "a thimble full is all you need". He opened the drawer under the bench and pulled out the parchment and the thimble. He had seen his dad put them there and told him not to lose them. He pulled out the thimble and dipped it in the water. It was so small; it was hard to hold on to.

"Man, that water is cold! It sure tastes good. Even though it's like putting a couple drops on your tongue as a teaser," said Bob aloud.

He waited for something to happen, nothing. No tingling, no shock, nothing. Bob let the fountain run, at the same time wondering how it could be possible.

Another week went by before Bob began to notice things that were not normal. He had shaved his beard that morning when he took the thimble of water. His beard hadn't grown since then and he normally had a shadow after three days. He was beginning to think there was something to this fountain's powers. Then he shrugged it off, shaking his head in disbelief.

Tom came home and left a few times between the three weeks. Bob decided to tell him what he had done, the thimble of water and the beard.

Tom reached over and rubbed his son's cheek. "That is unbelievable."

Both men sat there staring at the fountain and watching the drips of water slowly fall from the leaves. Then Bob looked at his dad and asked, "Hey, when did you start getting grey on the temples?"

"What do you mean? I'm too young to get any grey hair," replied Tom.

Just then Cathy walked into the room. "What's my two fellers doing?" she asked.

Bob blurted out, "Dad's getting grey!"

"Where?" asked Cathy.

"On his temples," added Bob.

Cathy looked at her husband and then at Bob. "He's just getting old, like his dad. Remember, that's the way his father started. By the way have you guys looked at the tree outside the building? I think someone needs to water it."

"What do you mean?" asked Tom getting up and heading towards the door. "It's just because we haven't had any rain in a couple weeks. I'll get the bucket and water it. Wait a minute, I never noticed the Hibiscus tree, but it does look like it is turning brown, towards the side facing the house. After that, it's green."

Bob walked out with his dad. "Need any help?" asked Bob pushing the fountain back towards the middle of the table. Tom looked over at his son and beyond him to the table, which held the fountain.

"You still messing with that fountain? You told me you were drinking the thimble of water. You are worse than your mother and her essential oils. Anything that feels different?" asked Tom.

Bob shrugged his shoulders, "Not really".

Cathy spoke up and told Tom that every time Bob drank from that little fountain of water, she noticed something about the air around them, like an invisible fog.

Tom stood there with his mouth open and after staring at Cathy, said "really?"

Bob went over to the fountain and took his dose of thimble water. Cathy and Tom both started rubbing their arms as if they had a cold chill. She knew the fog was getting stronger.

Tom on the other hand, was stunned at first. "I see what you mean. Sorry I didn't believe you before."

All at once, Cathy started coughing. It was a deep cough coming from her lungs, not just a clearing of the throat. She put her hand on the table and leaned over coughing to the point of almost vomiting.

Tom came over and put his hand on her back. "Honey, you alright?" Of course, Cathy wasn't alright. She was coughing so hard, that her chest was beginning to knot up from the intensity. Then she went limp in Tom's arms.

"Bob!" yelled Tom. "Call an ambulance, something is wrong with your mom!"

Bob had gone outside to help his dad with the watering, but Tom stayed inside when he heard Cathy coughing so persistently. Bob ran inside and headed for the phone.

Tom was holding Cathy now. She was still coughing and he also started to cough. But told Bob he was ok, just clearing his throat.

Bob knew better. Something was wrong. He thought maybe a gas leak or something. But why wasn't he affected? He called the ambulance and then helped his dad get his mom out of the building. He took her out front and was headed towards a park bench they had put outside. As Tom set Cathy down on the bench, he noticed she quit coughing. He asked her how she was and she replied, "fine now, I guess. I don't know what happened. I started getting weak and then the coughing started. I thought I was going to die!"

Tom didn't tell Cathy, but he had felt weak also. He had started coughing but tried to suppress it the best he could. He told Bob to call back the ambulance and tell them it was a false alarm and to cancel. Tom knew the ambulance would have taken about fifteen minutes to get there, so he felt he had time to call them before they were very far.

"Bob, did you spray the Hibiscus trees for bugs or something? The tree out here is half dead and I noticed the one out back was that way too. That might be what was making us cough so hard." added Tom. "I think we need to close the place up and have it checked out for chemicals, gas leak or whatever. We can go stay at the hotel for a couple days till it gets cleared."

Cathy and Bob agreed. They packed some clothes as quickly as they could. Bob went to the fountain and dumped the water. Why, he didn't know, but felt like it might have something to do with all this.

Later that week, as he walked towards the cafe, he didn't utter a word. The toxicity test finally came back. Everything was normal and Bob was still curious. He asked aloud to no one. "Why was the Hibiscus tree behind the building half dead and what caused his mom to have a coughing spell?"

He decided to go into the back room where he had set the fountain. There it was dry, but something wasn't right. As he got closer, Bob saw the vines coming out of the tiny holes. They were headed for the gallon of water that Bob had brought home for it.

"Oh no you don't!" yelled Bob as he grabbed the container and took it to the sink and poured it down the drain. The vines retracted as he started to walk towards it.

"What can I do with this?" Bob thought to himself. Then he remembered that old freezer out behind the station. He thought that would be a good place for it.

Bob had no symptoms like his mom or dad. In fact, he felt better than normal. Then he grabbed the fountain. There was a tingling feeling and it felt as if his strength was being pulled from him. Bob took it and shoved the thimble up inside as far as it could go with the piece of parchment paper that came with it. He knew it was just a piece of paper but he wasn't taking any chances.

Taking it outside, he opened the old freezer's door. There was a squeak that came from the hinges as the door opened fully. He started to place the fountain inside but he felt a presence behind him. He turned in time to see a tall dark figure, dressed in a black cloak with the hood pulled down to cover his face. His cloak went all the way to the ground covering his feet. It raised its arm, or what Bob thought to be an arm, and was pointing at the fountain. Bob stepped away from the freezer. Reaching out, the figure touched the fountain and both disappeared.

Those last two lines of the poem kept going through Bob's head.
"One last warning you must hear
Your youth draws strength from things so near."

Tom and Cathy had talked about selling their home, the café and station. They had never felt comfortable there after the incident. They asked Bob first if he had wanted the place. His answer was an immediate no. He liked the place however; he had not felt comfortable in it himself since the ordeal with the dark figure. That was something he had never discussed with his parents and probably never would. He was greatly relieved that they both had recovered completely.

The End?

Tom had finally sold the place to the first buyer. It took six months before he had someone say they were interested. He didn't care about a big profit, he just wanted out. A young couple by the names of Martha and Marion bought the place and decided to call it the "Double M".

A week after they purchased the property, Marion was out checking over his investment and found the old freezer. It was locked with a padlock. He pulled on it and decided to get a hammer and use it as a key.

It only took three tries before the padlock broke free. Marion put the hammer on the ground and opened the lid. Martha was inside the cafe cleaning hoping they could open in a few days. She heard the banging of the hammer and decided to go see what Marion was doing.

"Look what I found!" said Marion, holding his new treasure high in the air.

In that freezer was…

Made in the USA
Middletown, DE
13 June 2025

76978918R00135